Undercover Lover

First printing: March 2020
ISBN: 978-1-7339577-4-8
M.A.Rose
amazon.com/author/meganrosales

Acknowledgements

This book would not have been possible without the collaboration of Pamela Lopez. Many thanks, for your shared suggestions and ideas to help bring this story to life.

Chapter 1: Stella

"On your left!" I shout, but my partner is too slow and gets shot. I make a beeline for some stacked boxes to provide me with coverage, until I can catch my breath. "Come out, come out, wherever you are." I hear Mason taunt me. I pull out my compact mirror to see if I can get a view on my target. He's approaching from behind and to the right. I wait till he's a few feet away and I knock the boxes over. The distraction startles him long enough for me to shoot him. "Bang" I say as I stand over him with my gun pointed at his head.

"Ugh, I almost had you Stella." Mason says frustratingly as he kicks one of the boxes. The lights in the training room come on as I help, Jessie, my assigned partner up. "Almost," I say as I give him a smirk and turn in my training gun. "Good work today Jessie. You're improving quickly." "Really? Thanks Stella. I hope to be as good as you one day." She says admirably. Jessie is training to be one of our new operatives and she has been stuck to me like glue. I let out a chuckle, "Keep up the hard work and practice. Then who knows, you could be even better than me." I tell her in hopes of instilling some confidence. She sure is tenacious but she lacks the confidence, as most new trainees do. However, it's better than her being overconfident and thinking she's hot shit. Ron, our supervisor hates trainees like that and more often than not, fires them before they even graduate from training if they don't change their attitude around quick.

Nothing like a mid afternoon training course to get the

adrenaline going I think to myself. I head to the locker room to shower and change back into my work clothes. I make my way back to my office and try to suppress the smile that forms on my face as I enter my office and see the nicely polished name plate that reads *Stella Parks, International Secret Intelligence Agent*. Which is a mouthful, so we just call ourselves ISIA's. I work for the Global Anti-Corruption Force or GACF and I just got a promotion. So now I have my very own office and for some reason the name plate makes it all the more official. Since my promotion, I'm now tasked with training and molding some of the new hires that Ron feels has the utmost potential to excel in their class. "If only they could all be just like the Stellar Stella." Ron told me when he promoted me, even though he knows I hate that nickname.

I've worked hard to get where I'm at and it gives me a sense of pride. Growing up I bounced from foster home to foster home, not ever having a place to call home. I was always trying to be exactly what the families expected me to be and then when I didn't meet their expectations I was told I'd never amount to anything. Although it gave me a rugged mindset from an early age, it also helped attribute to what makes me the great agent I am today. I can swiftly adapt to any situation and I definitely don't need to rely on anyone. When I turned eighteen I was kicked out of the system. I was in Virginia at the time and I quickly got a job as a waitress and then a second job as a night shift housekeeper for a hotel. When I had enough money saved up, I went to college and majored in International Affairs and minored in French and

Spanish. After I graduated I decided to stay in Virginia and get a job under the Operations branch of the GACF, but quickly realized my need for the hands on aspect of gathering intel. I didn't want to be sitting on the sidelines while someone else did the dirty work for me, so I cross trained as an ISIA. I had many people tell me there's no way I'd make it, but look at me now, sitting in my own office with a fancy ass name plate teaching aspiring new agents. I wasn't always respected the way I am today. Other agents would taunt me and spread rumors that I slept with the supervisors and directors to get ahead, but I think that's because they can't handle the fact a girl could actually be better than them. The only agent that takes me as a serious competitor is Mason. That's why he always offers to run the training courses with me, in hopes of one day beating me. I also think he might still be a little hung up on me too. We had a fling for a couple months shortly after we both became agents, but I made it clear that I wanted to focus on my career.

All I know is, I love my job and I've busted my ass to get where I am today and no one can take that away from me. I guess what sets me apart is I'm not some cocky agent with an over inflated ego. I take my job seriously, but I also enjoy it, unlike some. Since I've joined the GACF I've been on numerous missions across the world and have picked up on a few more languages. I can't wait for my next mission though. Since I've been promoted they've been sending other agents out on missions while I sit here at a desk doing paperwork and it's driving me insane.

I sort through the remaining files and mark the ones of those who passed their physicals this week. I let out a large sigh as I swivel around in my chair. I've already done all my work for the week and it's only Wednesday. I'm itching to go on another mission. It's been three months since my last one and I've had more than enough time to rest and readjust to society. There's so many rules about how much time between missions that we are supposed to have. Laying low for for some time after a mission helps prevent our true identities from being discovered. This is a crucial part in our career field, if your cover is blown it can lead to serious consequences, if not death.

A hard knock at my door disrupts me from my thoughts. "Come in." I say. Mason pops his head around the corner with a devilish grin. "Yes, Mason?" "Just thought I'd let you know to try not to miss me too much while I'm gone." He tells me. "Doubtful. Where are you going?" I ask him while trying to hide my jealousy. "Now, now, Stella. We both know mission details are top secret." I roll my eyes, "Yeah, yeah. Stay safe agent Palmer." I tell him. "Roger that." He says before disappearing. Even though I wasn't all heart eyes for Mason, I didn't exactly hate him either, and I definitely would never wish any danger to him. It's just simple code of conduct to at least tolerate your co-agents.

When the clock hits five, I gather my things and leave for the day. I head to meet my jiu-jitsu instructor to continue my training like I do every Wednesday. I like to be well versed in my combat skills, because it reassures me that I can defend myself in most situations. I've done all kinds of martial arts throughout the years and it's really helped discipline and ground me.

"Hello Stella. "Hello Sensei" I say as I bow to Hitoshi, my jiu-jitsu instructor. "Are you ready to continue with your lesson?" He asks me. "I'm always ready." I tell him. He lets out a small laugh, "Indeed you are." The next hour I spend learning and practicing some illegal moves that would not count in matches, but serve as good defense mechanisms for me. Hitoshi is a skilled yet practical instructor. Even though I can't disclose what I do for a living, Hitoshi knows that my job requires a significant knowledge of self defense and fighting, but knows better than to ask questions. So he modifies my lesson plans to what he thinks will be beneficial to my line of work. Despite my secrets and reserved personal life, I consider Hitoshi as one of my close friends. When we finish, we bow to one another and then do some cool down stretches. "Will I see you next week Stella?" Hitoshi asks me. "I'll let you know by Tuesday." I tell him. He just nods and we part our ways.

When I make it home Kat, my best friend, greets me with a plate of spaghetti. "Just in time, dinner's ready." Kat says cheerfully. "Smells great." I tell her. We sit down at our table to eat and discuss minor details of work. It's nice having someone I can actually decompress and discuss work with. Me and Kat were in the foster system together and happened to be in and out of group homes together. She's been the one constant thing in my life and we bicker and love each other just like sisters. We pushed each other through college and I even helped her get a job on with the GACF.

She works in the cybersecurity department, so she works with computers and whatnot. Neither of us can talk specifics about our jobs so it's nice that we both understand and respect each others privacy. When I go on a mission, I just tell her how long I'm expected to be gone and she knows not to ask too many questions or try and contact me. Plus it's nice having some sort of social interaction with another person. It's hard to maintain or even start friendships with people when your a spy. I mean, secrecy and lies aren't exactly a good foundation for any friendship or relationship. Luckily, me and Kat share a special bond that started way before we even joined the GACF.

When we finish eating I retire to the living room, plop down on the couch and turn on the news. It's not the most pleasurable thing to watch, but it's important to stay up to date on current affairs in my profession. When the news is over I flip through the channels and find myself watching some sappy romance movie. I scoff out loud as the lady on the television falls into the man's arms at the perfect time and she thanks him for saving her. I guess I've just never had much luck in the love department, or dating in general and find it all a bit overrated. Most of the guys I've gone on dates with don't like my strong mindset or the fact I can hold my own. Let's not forget the fact that it's difficult to have an intimate relationship with someone when you can't tell them what you do for a living and occasionally disappear for months or years at a time without a trace. The only way to have a half way functioning relationship is with another agent, which is against the rules. Love and emotions can interfere with and even compromise a mission.

Chapter 2: Stella

The next morning I leave for work and stop to get a coffee on the way. I usually try to avoid feeding into addiction, but coffee is just so damn good. Once I have my coffee, I head to work. I'm curious what the day will hold. I know there's another training scheduled for this morning, but I wonder who will be running it now that Mason is gone.

When I walk into my office, I see Ron perched against my desk looking at my graduation photo. "Good morning Ron." I say. "Good morning Emma, so glad you could make it in today." Ron tells me with a smile. A big grin spreads across my face. An alias, this must mean I'm set for another mission. "Where's the file? I can't wait to start studying it." I tell him eagerly. He laughs, "Relax, we'll get there. This mission is a little more complicated than the others, I was saving it for you." "Ooh a challenge, I'm intrigued sir." "You say that now, but I'm afraid you aren't going to be so eager once you are fully briefed." "How so?" I question. "For starters, you will have a partner on this mission." Damn, a partner. Ron knows I like working solo, but if this one requires a partner then so be it. "Not a problem sir. You know I will always do what I must for the success of the mission." "Very well. From here on out you will be referred to as Emma Matthews. We will get you briefed on your new identity after training." "Copy that. Who will be performing the training with me today?" I ask Ron, but he walks off without answering me.

I meet Jessie in the locker room and she is bright and bushy tailed, per usual. "I reviewed my weak points from

yesterday and I am feeling much more confident for today."
She tells me. "Good, but remember, not every situation will
be the same so you must adapt to the situation as you go.
Trying to approach each situation the same way each time
can lead to a failed mission, the enemy getting away, injury,
or even death." I tell her sternly. "Got it." She says giving me
a firm nod. I'll have to remember to mark her down for
accepting of constructive criticism.

We collect our guns and post out. The lights shut off and
I quickly retrieve the night vision scope from my vest. Jessie
mimics me. Hopefully she's quicker on her feet this time. I
motion for us to advance forward. I'm trying to teach Jessie
to secure a position from behind the enemy that way she can
implement a sneak attack. It's bold and dangerous, so not
many agents go for such a tactic. When we make it to the
opposite end of the room, I finally spot the target slowly
advancing his way to where we just came from. Clever. He
has the same mindset as me, except he is going straight up
the middle when it's safer to go along the outside. I motion
for Jessie to take his left flank as I take his right. We slowly
inch our way toward him, but just as Jessie lines up for her
shot she steps on some glass and exposes herself. He quickly
draws his gun up in her direction, but I knock his arm up
causing him to miss his shot and I quickly disarm him. He
swiftly knocks me off my feet and I land on my back
stunned, but I quickly counter react and use my feet to take
him down to the ground. Once on the ground he tries to
wrestle me into a hold, but I beat him to it and get him into
submission so he has no choice but to tap out. Once I feel his

tap of defeat I roll off of him. I am curious to see which agent actually gave me a run for my money.

When the lights turn on I look over at the mystery man and it's not an agent I recognize. Surely this isn't a trainee that wiped me off my feet. If so he's a damn good one. He's tall, tan, and buff, but still looks lean. I am studying his short dark hair and his hazel eyes when Ron emerges from the viewing booth and gives us an applause. "Emma Matthews I see you've met your husband, Derek Matthews." Ron tells me as he motions toward the man I just trained with. I know better than to argue, so I give him a smile. Apparently he will be my partner for this mission and our cover is as husband and wife. We shake hands. "Nice work Derek." I compliment. "You too. Not too shabby for a girl." He teases. I grit my teeth to hold back what I really want to say. "If I recall, you're the one who tapped out." I tell him. He may be handsome, but if he's really this arrogant then this is going to be a long mission. "Shower up and meet me in the briefing room" Ron tells us.

I quickly shower and head straight to the briefing room. I am ready to get my file and prepare for the mission. I take a seat and Derek, my partner arrives shortly after me. Ron and another man I never saw before enters the room. The man and Derek nod to one another and I rise from my chair to greet the man. "Emma Matthews." I say introducing myself. "Nice to meet you Emma. I am Randall Brown, head of the undercover agents for the FBI." He says as he shakes my hand. "Pleasure to meet you sir." I say as I take my seat once again. "Now that you two have met, it's time to move forward with details regarding your assignment. Here are your files for the identities you two are taking. Study them, know them, be them. This will be who you are for the next six months, if all goes according to plan." Ron tells us as he hand us the folders. "I'm sure you are curious as to why you are being partnered with an FBI agent." Mr. Brown says to me. "This is because, the mission you will be going on will be under unofficial orders. As a GACF agent, if you are apprehended or exposed, we would not be able to rescue you or transfer you back to the U.S., which means you would be prosecuted in their country. By going with an FBI agent this eliminates those risks and will grant you protection. You also have no law enforcement capabilities, Derek here can apprehend the men we are after if the opportunity presents itself and call for back up if needed." I give Randall a nod to show that I understand.

The next hour they spend briefing us on a proclaimed terrorist group in Russia, that have been more frequently producing threats against the United States. The leader of the group, Viktor Chubinsky, is a known mafia member who use to live in the U.S. and recently moved back to Russia after setting up an underground drug and weapon smuggling ring. The FBI has had a hard time nailing these guys on the state side, which is probably why they are sending us over there. The group is now claiming they have some heavy duty weapons and some nuclear access that they plan to use on the United States. Our job, is to get solid physical evidence of Viktor Chubinsky's involvement in the drug and weapon smuggling ring. Once we have this intel, Derek can call in for the arrest. If possible, we need to determine how serious their threats to the U.S. are as well.

As far as covers go, Derek and I are newly weds, honeymooning in Russia while Derek inquires about setting up an international branch for his foreign trade business. If all goes to plan, Viktor will be interested in doing business with Derek and send his henchmen to suggest doing so. This will allow us to get on the inside and gather the intel we need.

"Now Emma, I know it's not in your nature, but this mission requires you to be submissive and not outspoken. You must play the role of an obedient woman who listens to whatever her husband says." Ron tells me. I give him a daggering look. At least he warned me the mission would be challenging. "Anything else?" I ask him. "Actually yes," he tells me. "We are either going to have to cut your hair or dye it." No, not my luscious wavy brown hair, I think to myself. "No cutting, we can dye it" I tell him firmly. I'm still trying to grow it back out after the last mission. "Very well, we will get you set up with the hairstylist to get it done." "Is there anything I need to do?" Derek asks. "No. You are fine the way you are." Ron tells him.

Once we finish getting briefed, they dismiss us and I head for the elevator. We have three days to study our identities and learn everything about our partners identity as well. That's why I plan on heading straight home and cozying up on my couch to study our files. "Hold the elevator!" Derek says as he jogs up. I stop the elevator and he gets in the elevator with me. "Thanks wifey." Derek says to me. I just roll my eyes. "Did you want to grab some lunch and get to know each other some?" He asks. "It's prohibited to discuss true identities, in case the mission is compromised and we are captured and tortured for intel." I tell him flatly. "I meant as our aliases. I feel it's always easier to remember the details when you learn them more naturally than reading up on them." He tells me. He has a point, but I'm trying to acclimate to this whole partner thing. "I don't think it's wise to discuss top secret details in a public setting." I tell him, which is also true. "Well I'm not from here so maybe I can come to your place? Maybe my wife will be nice enough to make me a sandwich, I'm starving." He says as he pats his belly. I inhale and exhale deeply as I ignore his sexist comment. I'm sure the comments will only get worse if he knows it bothers me. Plus, it could all be apart of the act too. I briefly read over his file and saw that he will be head of the household and will be *wearing the pants* in the relationship. It's hard to tell though. "Not today." I tell him as I get off the elevator. "Is this our first fight?" He shouts after me. I'm glad my back is turned, because his last comment actually gets me to crack a smile.

The next day I meet with Brooke, one of our talented stylists to start my dreaded makeover. "I can't believe you're actually going to let me dye your hair." Brooke says. I give her a frown, "I have no choice. It was either that or cut it again." I tell her. "What a shame." She says while shaking her head. "Here have a seat while I go grab some of my things." She tells me.

As I'm waiting for her to return, I hear the door open and look to see who it is. "Derek, what are you doing here?" I ask him. "Thought I could come keep my babe some company while she gets pampered." He tells me. I cringe when he calls me babe. "Don't be silly. I'll be just fine without your company." I reply. "Ouch" he says as he clenches his heart dramatically.

"Why hello." Brooke says as she reenters the room with her supplies. "Well hello yourself." Derek says to Brooke as he flashes her a pearly white grin. She lets out a flirtatious giggle. "And who might you be?" She asks him. Yuck, I can't believe I'm sitting here witnessing this. "Derek Matthews and you?" He asks. "Brooke, I'm one of the agency's stylists." "Well don't mind me. I'll let you work your magic on my lovely wife here." "Oh, I see." Brooke says as she shoots me a mischievous grin. "Surely there's something else you could be doing right now?" I say hastily. "What I can't watch you get your hair done? I think it's important that I'm able to recognize my wife, don't you?" He asks rhetorically. "Whatever" I mutter.

"Alright let's get started." Brooke tells me. "So what are you thinking?" I ask her. "Well you have such a nice brown color that I don't want to totally destroy by going blonde. Plus that will take time to titrate the color down." She tells me. I nod my head to show my comprehension. "I think going too dark won't go with your skin tone very well either." Brooke adds. "So what does that mean?" I ask "I'm thinking we should go red." Brooke tells me. "A redhead?" I shriek. Derek lets out a chuckle and makes his presence all the more annoying. Brooke gives me a frown, "Well unless you have a better idea?" She tells me. "No, no. I trust you. I just never saw myself as a redhead." I tell her. "I think it fits you, you're feisty." Derek comments. "No one asked you." I snap. Derek throws his hands up in the air, "See my point exactly." He says. "This is going to take a couple hours at least." Brooke tells me. I let out a groan, at least I brought the files to go over. Derek looks at his watch, "Welp, I guess I'll check back in a little bit so you two can have some girl talk." I roll my eyes and Brooke lets out a chuckle.

Once Derek disappears, Brooke swivels my chair to face her. "Um, hello hottie," she exclaims. I just shake my head and laugh. "Excuse me? You cannot tell me that you don't think mister tall, dark, and handsome is attractive?" She asks while giving me a bewildered look. "I mean, yeah he's easy on the eyes, but he's kind of an arrogant asshole. I want someone with more than just looks." I tell her. "Good point. I guess I wouldn't mind being stuck with him as my pretend husband though." Brooke says as she swivels me back around and starts working on my hair. "Eh. Could be better, could be worse." I say. "I hope he's a good kisser for your sake." She says while letting out another giggle. "Brooke!" I exclaim, while my face turns red from embarrassment. "Okay, okay. I'm done. It's time to get to work." She tells me. I then retrieve my file from my bag and do some studying while she works on my hair.

Chapter 3: Liam

Damn, I can't tell if Emma genuinely finds me annoying or is just playing hard to get. I try to shake the thought from my head, because it doesn't matter. I shouldn't be worried about what she thinks. She's my partner and that's all there is to it, but it's important that we seem compatible. Otherwise, Chubinsky and his guys will see right through our cover.

It's apparent she doesn't take well with the submissive role. I can tell she's a strong independent woman and I admire that. That's not the only thing I admire either. If it wasn't so unprofessional, I would thank Randall for partnering me with one sexy lady. She's short and petite, so maybe 5'4' and 130lbs max. It's obvious she takes care of herself and works out too. She has medium chocolate brown hair and beautiful blue eyes that can entrance a helpless soul. She is also spunky, sassy, and straightforward. I would not want to be on her bad side. Nothing like Anna, the woman my parents want me to marry.

I'm stoked that I get to pretend that Emma is my wife and can't wait to start the mission with her. I just wish she would open up some. She's really reserved and quiet. Maybe that's just how she is? I've always tried to be outgoing and open, which is not necessarily the best qualities for an agent, but I think it makes me seem more trustworthy and personable. Being too reserved can be suspicious to certain people and make missions way more difficult.

My phone starts to buzz. I pull out my personal cell and see that it's Anna calling. I let out a huff. I've told her multiple times not to call me while I'm away for work. I turn my cell phone off and put it away, I can't afford any distractions while I'm preparing for the mission at hand. I can't believe my parents are really trying to strong arm me into marrying this girl. Just because Pa works with her dad at the White House they think we are a perfect match. She's a superficial gold digger. She's also twenty-three, that's six years younger than me and it just feels weird. I mean she's cute I'll give her that and she can hold a decent conversation, but we don't share many interests. Maybe if she was more mature like Emma, it wouldn't be as bad. Now I catch myself wondering how old Emma is. The good thing about these files is that some of this information is a true testament to the agents likes, dislikes, age, and so forth. Only things that are actually traceable are altered. For instance their age is accurate but their birthdate is made up. I pick up her file and scan through, until I find her age. Twenty six, see that's perfect. Stop it, quit thinking about her like that I tell myself.

Ma and Pa have been stressing that it's about time for me to settle down and start a family, but they don't understand that my job is my life. I've done my part by walking the straight and narrow and living a plain life in order to help Pa look good. I did what I was told and got a respectable degree and then worked my way up to an FBI agent. My parents originally wanted me to go into politics, since they were convinced that Pa could get my foot in the door with his ties to the White House, but it doesn't really peak my interest. When I grew up and found out that Pa is a part of the secret service, it only made me want to be badass agent myself. Even though I know Pa could've easily referred me, I didn't want to take a job under the impression that I only got the job because my dad has connections. I wanted to prove my worth, so, I applied for the FBI academy and worked my way up to a field agent. Pa's feelings were hurt, but it fulfilled my sense of pride to know I got to where I am today all on my own.

After an hour of studying Emma's file, I discover that she loves coffee, so I determine that it might be a good time for a coffee break. I take a stroll down to the coffee shop around the corner and get us both a coffee. I head back to the styling department and hope that she appreciates the small gesture and doesn't think I'm trying to hit on her. For all I know she could have boyfriend, or hell, a husband.

When I enter the room I see her sitting in the same chair, but now she has a bunch of foil in her hair. She still looks pretty damn cute though. I refrain from laughing and poking fun at her since I know that aggravates her. "Mmm, is that coffee?" Emma asks as she sniffs the air. "Sure is. Four pumps vanilla cream and two packs of sugar, just the way you like." I tell her. "Seriously?" She asks, almost surprised that someone would do such a thing. "Yeah, all yours." I say as I hand her the cup. She takes the cup and looks at me suspiciously, before taking a sip. "Ahh." She exclaims after taking a long sip. "Did I get it right?" I ask. "Yes, you did. What do I owe you?" Emma asks. "Nothing. I just figured we could both use a mid afternoon pick me up." I tell her. "Well, maybe you're not so bad after all." Emma teases. Who knew all it took to lighten her up is some coffee, and was that a smile I saw? Maybe now we can start moving forward with getting to know each other.

Chapter 4: Stella

I admit I was skeptical at first as to why Derek would bring me a coffee for no reason. I've just never had a guy surprise me with a gift out of genuine kindness before and it feels weird. Maybe he's not as terrible as I've previously thought? I feel bad for being so harsh with him, but it's just hard for me to open up to people. I need to put my fears and doubts aside and learn to connect with people, starting with Derek.

I see him start to get antsy as if his presence is unwelcome and turns to leave. "When did we get married?" I quiz him. He turns around swiftly, "October fourth of this year. You always dreamed of a fall wedding." Oh he's good. "What college did I go to?" He asks. "Wharton school of business through the University of Pennsylvania. All hail your father's alma mater." I say matching his commitment. He gives me an approving nod. I can't think of another question so he quickly asks another. "What are your parent's names?" For some reason his question throws me off and I find myself wanting to tell him about my true past, but I'm sure he doesn't care about me and my charity case of a life. "Ryan and Maisy Clark. I tell him. "My turn." I say before he can ask another question. "What's my favorite flower?" "Hmm, I'd have to guess Dahlia's." "There is no way you could just guess that and get it right. Especially when it's true." I say astonished. "Why not?" Derek says. "Because do you know how many flowers there are? And for you to accurately guess the one type that happens to be my favorite, which isn't even a common one, is highly unlikely." I tell him. "Well I don't know what to tell you. When I looked at you, I thought of the prettiest flower that I could emulate such beauty." He tells me. I can't tell if it's a part of the act or if he's actually hitting on me, but it's doubtful. Guys don't look at me that way, and when they have it's only for one thing, sex. "Alright, game over." I tell him. "Why? Are you mad that you can't read people as good as me?" He asks. "What? No. I'm just starting to get a headache from the fumes I've been inhaling. No offense Brooke." I say. "None taken girl." Brooke tells me. "How much longer anyway?" Derek says impatiently, as if he's being forced to stay and watch. "All that's left is to wash and blow dry it." Brooke says excitedly.

Brooke leads me over to the hair wash station and proceeds to wash my hair. When she's finished we move back to the chair for her to blow dry my hair. I get nervous as she starts to dry it. I hope I don't look silly with red hair. I close my eyes because I can't handle the anticipation. "Alright, take a look." Brooke says when she's finished. Derek lets out a catcall, "My wife is on fire!" His comment forces me to open my eyes. As I look in the mirror, I admire Brooke's handiwork. Not bad, I am relieved to see that I can pull off the redhead look. "Do you like it?" Brooke asks. "Actually, I really do." I tell her while giving her an appreciative smile which prompts her to give me a small hug.

I collect my things and meet Derek at the door. I'm not really sure what's going on. He's been waiting around as if we have plans or something, but there's nothing scheduled on our agenda. "Well, thanks for the coffee and company." I tell Derek. He gives me a slight nod. I'm sure he has finally realized how socially awkward I am. Good going Stella, I think to myself. We both stand in silence for a brief moment until Derek clears his throat. "So uh, Emma. As I've mentioned before. I'm not from around here and was curious if you knew any good places to may grab lunch or dinner?" I can tell he's trying to reach out and I've just been a reserved asshole. Time to break out of your comfort zone Stella Parks. "Yeah. It just kind of depends on what your wanting though." I tell him. "I've been craving a juicy burger and some fries." He tells me. "I know just the place." I say. "You can ride with me" I add. His face lights up and I can tell my change of attitude has already made a difference. For some reason, I find it satisfying to know that I made him happy, but why?

On the way to the restaurant we quiz each other some more over our identities and discuss standard tactics that we feel will be beneficial to the case. It's going to be interesting to see how we function as a unit. Since I've never had a partner before, I have to get use to not always calling the shots on my own. I also have to get use to the concept that from now, until the end of the mission, I am married and I need to start acting like it. Otherwise, we are going to stick out like a sore thumb in Russia. Ron's already pulled me aside and told me I need to do my best to get my shit together. I've never had a serious relationship before. When Mason and I were together it had to be a secret so it's not like we could go on dates and do actual things couples do. It was always quick mid-day hook ups and late night booty calls.

After we order our food, I think of a very forward idea I want to run by Derek. "So Derek, I was thinking about what you said." I tell him. He gives me a puzzled expression. "Emma, I say a lot of things." He tells me as he lets out a chuckle. "About getting acquainted with each other more naturally instead of just reading a file." "Ah, yes I remember now." He says. "Well, I've never had a partner before." "Really, I couldn't tell." He interjects, while giving me a smirk. "Stop it, I'm being serious." I tell him. "Okay, I'm sorry. Continue." He says. "And to be quite frank, I've never been in a serious relationship" I say as look down at the ground, trying to hide my embarrassment. You are a strong woman, I tell myself, now act like it. I straighten up and bring my shoulders back, "Therefore, I was hoping we could start acting as if we are actually in a relationship. That way I can get accustomed to the whole process and idea." I tell him. He grabs ahold of my hand and I try to instantly pull away, but he only squeezes my hand tighter. I meet his gaze and he's looking right at me as he lets out a soft laugh. "Well for starters babe, you're gonna have to get use to physical affection." Derek says followed with a wink. I'm not sure if it's his wink or his words that trigger goosebumps to form all over my body, making me feel as if I'm a pathetic horny teenager all over again. He finally lets my hand go and I retreat it back to my side. Have I really just been deprived of physical affection that long, to were my body is sensitive to Derek's mere touch? "So I take that as a yes?" I ask him. He sits back in his chair and rubs his chin as if he's thinking it over. I give him glare which causes him to laugh, "Easy killer. Of course I'm down. I just feel like this is going to be a bit difficult for you." I let out a scoff, "What's that supposed to mean?" I ask. "You already admitted you don't have any experience in the dating department and it's like you're closed off to any human connection." Even though I know what he's saying is true, it still strikes a nerve. "Well excuse me for not being well versed in the love department. Not all of us grew up in an environment filled with love, warmth, and all that wholesome living shit." I tell him. He just stares at me and now I feel silly for airing out my insecurities to basically a stranger who could care less. "All I'm saying is, it's going to be a bit more challenging for you since you aren't as comfortable with the whole idea. I think it's a great idea that you want to start the act before we get over there."He tells me. I simply nod, I feel as if I've said enough. "Just play along and follow my lead until you get the hang of it." He tells me comfortingly. "Alright." I tell him.

The next day we go through our authentication process. This is the time consuming part. We get all of our falsified documents, like our IDs, degrees, marriage certificate, really anything to support our identities. We also get our assigned cell phones, social media accounts, and have to perform a photoshoot to get photos to support our identities lives. "This will be a good time to play along with the relationship thing, otherwise this is just going to be an awkward photoshoot for you." Derek tells me. "I'll try." I tell him.

They start by splitting us up and and doing photos with our fake families and some individual photos for major accomplishments. This takes awhile itself because we have to change clothes, style our hair differently, and switch out props so it doesn't look suspicious. Our editors do a great job adding backgrounds and making some of the photos look really candid. I'm always impressed with the results.

"Alright now we'll have you two together. We're going to start with the first date and work our way all the way up to the wedding." Kathy, one of the photographers tells us. I go back to my dressing room as one of the stylists hands me an outfit to change into. I let out a deep breath. You can do this. Just let loose and have fun, I say trying to convince myself. I quickly get dressed and emerge from the dressing room. I approach Derek and he gives me a big smile.

"There's my beautiful wife!" Derek exclaims as he extends his arm out. I hesitate at first, but wrap my arm around his as he leads me to a bench. The photographers prompt us to take some selfies on our phones before we switch positions and take some more. Then we change and take some more casual photos together and some with our *friends* before we change again and take holiday photos with each others families. I actually find myself enjoying the whole process. It helps that everyone is so laid back and having fun with it too.

It's not until Kathy announces that it's time for us to prepare for the wedding shoot that I get nervous all over again. I head to my dressing room for the last time. A couple girls from the styling department crowd around me to get started on my makeup. I've always been a minimalist when it comes to makeup. Not because I don't like wearing it, but because half way through the day it's all smeared or sweated off, leaving me to look like a wild raccoon. When they finish I commend the natural yet glamorous look they produced for me. Brooke then finds me and goes over different styling options for my hair. We agree on a fancy partially braided updo with some flowers added into the mix. Next they assist me with getting into the beautiful princess style wedding dress that is provided. I adore the lacy quarter sleeves that give it a traditional look, but also admire the crystals elegantly placed along the dress giving it some modern appeal. I'm curious how much this dress cost. "Alright it's show time!" Kathy yells once she's informed that I'm finished getting ready.

With the help of the girls, I make my way back into the main room. "Wow, you look absolutely gorgeous!" Derek exclaims. Even though I know it's a part of the act, I can't help but blush. "You don't look so bad yourself." I reply, as I take account of his appearance. His hair is slicked back and he has on a black and white tux that molds to his muscular physique perfectly. "You sure you're ready to marry me?" He asks. "Hmm." I say as I tap my chin. "I don't have much of choice. This is an arranged marriage after all." I tell him. He laughs and I can't help but notice his strong jawline and flawless smile. I hate to admit it, but damn, he sure is handsome.

They start by handing us our rings and try to get photos of us putting them on one another. "Emma, you need to relax. You look too serious in these photos. Remember this is supposed to be the happiest day of your life." Kathy tells me frustratingly. I give her an apologetic nod. Derek takes my hand in his and gives me a warm smile. I smile back at him as he slides the ring on my finger. "Alright perfect. Now it's time for you two lovebirds to kiss." Kathy says. I let out a nervous chuckle as I look at Derek and then back at Kathy. "Waiting." Kathy says impatiently. Derek holds out his hand and I place my hand in his. In one swift motion Derek pulls my body to his and tilts me back while planting one long kiss on me. When his lips collide with mine, my body practically melts in his arms and I find myself in a lust struck daze, kissing him back. "Got it!" Kathy shouts. Derek's lips linger on mine for a second longer before he pulls me back to an upright position and releases me from his grip. I'm instantly breathless when he pulls away and I'm left feeling equally shocked, as I am pleased, at what just happened. For a brief second I forget where I'm at until I look around and see some of the girls giggling. I meet Derek's smoldering gaze and I wonder if he felt the same sizzling spark, or if this is just another day on the job for him? He's probably been through this same thing countless times with female partners and that's why he's so good at it. Derek leans into my ear, "Should we consummate the marriage now?" He whispers. His warm words instantly make me weak in the knees, but I maintain my composure as I punch him in the shoulder. "Ouch, I'm kidding." He says. "You better be." I say as I hike up my dress and stomp off to my dressing room.

Chapter 5: Liam

I'm officially an idiot, I think to myself. Emma was finally starting to open up and then I had to go and make a stupid comment like that. I can't help it though. She is hella gorgeous and being all dolled up in that wedding dress made her look even sexier. Damn and when we kissed, it took every fiber of my being to pull away. I've never felt such a spark when I've kissed someone before. I wonder if it was as magical for her as it was for me? I can't deny that kissing her made me want to take her home and do things I shouldn't ever think about doing with my partner. Maybe I should tell Randall that my attraction is too strong too Emma and I need to remove myself from the mission? That would mean no more Emma though and I don't know if I like the thought of that.

I don't want her thinking I'm just some slimy horn-dog so, I decide to wait for her outside her office to apologize. I can't deny that my mind hasn't wandered to what it would be like to sleep with Emma, but, there's something about her that makes me want more than just a sloppy one night stand. I want to know the real Emma. Starting with what her real name is. It's driving me insane with all these rules the GACF has in place for their agents. I would have no problem telling her my real name and getting to know her on a personal level, but the GACF prohibits any such thing as it may interfere with the mission. I can tell Emma is a stickler on the rules and takes her job seriously and that's why I'm not pushing her to go against protocol. She's a distinguished agent and I know from personal experience that it's hard work to build up a reputation. I've always wanted to find a woman who is devoted to her job as much as I am to mine. That way we can both work hard and play harder, if you get what I mean. Anna is always nagging how I'm never around, but with a woman like Emma, she would understand because she would be busting her ass at work too.

"Need something Derek?" Emma says, disrupting my thoughts. "Hey. Um, yeah I just wanted to apologize if I took it too far earlier, at the end of the photoshoot. I hope I didn't offend you." I tell her. "It's alright. I know you're just trying to help me get in the right mindset for the mission." She tells me. It makes me a little sad to know that she thinks my attraction for her is all just an act, but it's also a relief in case she doesn't feel the same way. "Right. Sometimes I just get a little carried away and I didn't want you getting the wrong idea." I reply. "Not at all. I know not to take anything you say to heart." Emma says. Shit, that's not how I wanted this conversation to go. "Well, I did mean it when I said that you looked gorgeous in that dress." I tell her. She looks away and I can tell I've made her uncomfortable. "Um, thanks." Is all she says. "Anyways, that's all. I just wanted to apologize, so you didn't think I was some weirdo." I tell her. "Too late." She tells me with a smile. I return the smile and decide to end the conversation here before I make this situation anymore awkward. "See you tomorrow." I say and then walk off.

I decide to call it an early night and head back to my hotel. I spend about an hour or so reviewing some of the files and building a good portfolio for my fake business that hopefully draws Chubinky's interest. I finally have to tell myself to give it a break before I pull out all of my hair. I fall onto the bed and pull out my personal cell. I turn it back on to see if Ma or Pa has tried to get ahold of me. Nope just a dozen missed calls from Anna. I toss my phone on the night stand and turn on the TV, but it doesn't take long for me to pass out.

A knock at the door wakes me, and I look at the clock, it reads midnight. Who in the world could that be? I get up and answer the door. "Emma, what are you doing here?" I ask surprised. She puts her finger to my lips and softly pushes me back into the room. I'm about to ask her if something is wrong when she lets her jacket fall to the ground, leaving her in nothing but lingerie. I feel myself harden at her exposed presence. She shoves me on the bed and climbs on top of me. She runs her hands up my shirt and cues me to take it off, so I do as she wishes. She makes a trail of kisses from my neck down to my pants and stops to undo my belt and unbutton my pants. She gives me a seductive gaze as she teases me with her hands. I pull her back on top of me and I'm just about to take her bra off when my phone rings.

My eyes open and I let out a groan at the realization that it was all just a dream. I roll over and pick up my phone. Of course it's Anna. I knew I'd kick myself for not turning my phone back off. I regretfully answer the call and spend the next hour listening to how I haven't answered any of her calls and how she had to go to a party by herself. Which made her look like a loser and blah, blah, blah. I'm sure she would have a hissy fit if she knew what I was really doing. I use to feel guilty for lying about my job and what I'm doing, but then I realized she doesn't really care. Plus you can't lie to someone when they don't even ask. Anna never asks about my job, or how my day was. She's only concerned when I'll be back and what I'm gonna do to make it up to her for being gone. Luckily, she's easily bought with a new purse or some new shoes and all is well in her world, because then she can post online her latest gift, claiming she's the luckiest girl in the world.

Chapter 6: Stella

I planned on working for another hour or so, but after all that's happened today, I'm not able to concentrate. I grab my things and head home. I can't wait to get home and tell Kat about this. I can already picture the shocked look on her face. I've never come home and confided in her about guy problems, but I have to get this off my chest. I have to keep in mind this is all a cover, but holy shit. That kiss was entrancing. I can't tell Kat all the details, but just enough to where maybe she can talk some sense into me. After all, I can't let one kiss distract me from what's really important, the mission.

"Hold up! That's him?" Kat practically yells when I show her one of the selfies we took today. "Yep." "So let me get this straight. Your next mission is to be away with this outrageously sexy guy for six months, while pretending to be his wife and today you two kissed and after just one kiss he has you all hot and bothered?" "Well I wouldn't go that far." I let out a chuckle. "Oh come on Stella. You said the kiss is all you've been able to think about since it happened. No guy has ever captivated the diligent Stella Parks like this before." "Exactly. That's why I'm worried." I tell Kat. "Why? Do you know how many girls would pay to be in your situation right now?" Kat tells me. "Because, my emotions could interfere with the mission at hand. Should I back out now?" I ask Kat. She gives me a flat stare. "You, back out of a mission? I never thought I'd hear those words come out of your mouth. Besides, I think you're overreacting. I think the fact you crave his physical affection would make your cover seem all the more real." Kat tells me. "Hmm. I didn't think about it that way, I guess that's a valid point." I tell her. "If you're worried about getting your lines skewed, distance yourself and set boundaries." Kat suggests. I let out a sigh, "I know. He made it clear that sometimes he gets carried away with his act and didn't want me to get the wrong impression." "He told you that himself?" "Yeah, he came to my office after the fact and apologized for a comment he made, because he didn't want me to think anything of it." She raises an eyebrow at me and I know she isn't satisfied with my vagueness. "After the kiss he whispered in my ear if we should consummate the marriage. But he was kidding, obviously." Kat lets out a squeal, "Omg, he totally wants you." "That's not true. He was pretty adamant about letting me know not to get the wrong impression. Hell, for all we know he could have a girlfriend or already be married." I tell Kat. "You realize I could have that answer in the matter of minutes." Kat says mischievously. "Absolutely not. Knowing personal details prior to a mission are against the rules." I tell her. "Fine." Kat says disappointedly as she sets down her laptop. "Now that we got that out of the way, I'm gonna go study for a bit before I head to bed." I tell her. "Is that what you call it?" Kat teases me. I just roll my eyes and walk off.

I allow myself to study for about an hour before I lay down for bed. My wandering mind keeps me from falling to sleep easily and I quickly become frustrated. I've never had a stupid guy get in my head like this before. What makes him so special anyway? There's plenty of pretty boys who flaunt about the agency that I don't even think twice about. Plus,

Derek told me himself not to get the wrong impression, yet here I am, laying awake thinking of him. That's it, I need to keep this strictly professional and that's it. I'll play along with the act, but that's all it is, an act, nothing more. When I see him tomorrow, I'm just going to go about my business as usual and not let his presence faze me.

The next morning I show up to work, ready to nail my objectives for the day. Today we will be individually interrogated and then afterwards we are set to attend a public event together to test our compatibility. If we pass both of these tests then they will mark us ready to move forward with the mission. I sure hope Derek brought his A-game, because I've never had to remediate before, and I don't plan on starting today.

When I make it to work, I head straight to the interrogation room and prep myself for a longer and much more intense game of 20 questions. As I enter the room, I see a cup of coffee with my name on it, sitting on the table. I take my seat and take a sip of the coffee. When just the right amount of vanilla and sugar hit my tastebuds, I realize the coffee is another gift from Derek. I catch myself smiling like an idiot and quickly try to erase my obvious display of gratification. Although it was kind of him to get me another coffee, it's probably his subliminal way of wishing me good luck.

A few minutes pass before Ron enters the room with the files and pulls up a chair across from me. There are only a select few times when Ron is a straight up hard ass and interrogations are one of those times. The next forty-five minutes he spends drilling me with questions all about mine and Derek's alias's. When we finish, I feel confident that I passed, but my nerves always fill my head a slight bit of self doubt. "Very good, now go get ready for your outing." Ron tells me once we are finished. I gather my things and make my way out the door. As I round the corner I run into Derek.

"Oh goodness. I'm so sorry." I say. "It's all good. At least the cup was empty." Derek says. I let out a small laugh, "Yeah, thanks for the coffee by the way." I tell him. He flashes me a smile, "No problem. How'd it go?" He asks. "Good, I guess. He told me to get ready for the outing, so that must mean I passed." I say. "Awesome. Well I better get in there. I'll catch up to you in a little bit" "Alright." I say as I step aside and let him pass. See that wasn't so hard. He's just a regular person.

I go to my office and drop off my things and then head to the styling department to borrow some clothes. As mine and Derek's last test, we have to attend a local charity auction. The kick is, there will be people watching me and Derek to see how well we function as a couple, which will determine how compatible we are for our cover. We won't know whose watching us so we have to be entirely invested. I help myself to a nice blouse and skirt off the rack to change into. When I'm finished, I pick out some nice heels and a peacoat to match my outfit and make my way back to the lobby to wait for Derek. I pull out my phone to text Kat that I'll be home late. It doesn't take long for her to respond.

Kat: *Ooh, late night rendezvous with the sexy good kisser?* Stella: *Lol, something like that.* Kat: *Tell him you two*

should practice kissing some more, for the sake of the job of course. I can't help but let out a chuckle before replying.
Stella: *We'll see, ttyl*

"What's so funny?" Derek asks, causing me to jump in my seat and fumble my phone. Jesus, how long had he been there? Hopefully he didn't see my conversation with Kat. "Um, nothing. Just my roommate being silly is all." "Ah. Shall we?" Derek asks as he offers his hand to help me up. "I can drive us." I tell him. "Sounds great. I could get use to you driving me around everywhere." He jokes. "Yeah until, I start charging you." I tease him. "It would be worth every penny." He says as he grabs my hand and holds it as we are walking. How is he so smooth? When we make it to the car he opens my door for me and then takes his place in the passenger seat.

We make small talk on the way to the event and when we arrive he orders me to wait and opens my door for me once more. As we are walking to the building he holds my hand again, and I'd be lying if I said I didn't enjoy it. Once in the building we are approached by a few of the organization leaders and we introduce ourselves.

"I'm Derek Matthews and this is my wife Emma." Derek says introducing us to the group. "Pleasure to meet you two. Thank you so much for coming, you don't know how much your support means." The lady in the middle tells us. "The pleasure is ours, ma'am. My husband is very passionate about your foundation. In fact, we were discussing how we would like to make a small contribution to your fund aside from the auction." I tell them. All three of their faces light up. "That is very generous of you Mr. and Mrs. Matthews. We would be happy to assist you with doing so." The bald headed gentleman says and then leads us to a lady who I would assume to be the treasurer of the organization, so we can make our payment. It's always nice coming to these things undercover, because the GACF credits us so we can make donations and payments without coming out of pocket.

After we make our payment we head back into the main gathering area to enjoy some hors d'oeuvres and drinks while mingling with some others. "That looks gross." Derek comments as I eat a stuffed mushroom. "They're really good. Wanna try one?" I ask him. "Eh. I don't know. Mushrooms are a fungus." Derek says squeamishly. "Ah, come on babe" I coo as I hold one up for him to take a bite, "do it for me." I plead. Derek reluctantly takes a bite of the mushroom and then swallows it. "Well what do you think?" I ask him. "I guess it's not terrible." He says. "Do you want the rest then?" I ask him. "I better not push it Em. My stomach doesn't react well to strange foods." I let out a snicker at the image of him running to the toilet later and then quickly realize he's already given me a nickname. How does bonding with someone come so natural for him? "I'm gonna go grab us some drinks, I'll be right back." Derek tells me. I watch him fade into the crowd before I start looking around. I notice some pretty prestigious people are at this event. I try to spot anyone who looks out of place so I can get an idea of who is watching us, but no such luck. I feel a tap on my shoulder and expect it to be Derek, but it's another man I've never seen before.

"Hi, I'm Zach." The guy says. "Emma." I say, as I shake his hand. "What's a pretty girl like you doing all alone?" Zach asks me. I never know how to respond to comments like that. After all, I didn't realize it was so unheard of for a woman to go into socialization without a man. I open my mouth so I can give the guy an ever so sassy response, until I feel a towering presence behind me. "Unfortunately for you, she's not alone." Derek says tensely before handing me a drink and puts his arm around me. "Thanks babe." I say as I look up at him with a smile. The guy doesn't even bother responding and just slinks off into the crowd. Even though I could easily tell the guy a piece of my mind, it was comforting to know Derek had my back. "Thanks for being there." I tell him. "Of course. You're my wife, I'll always be here for you." He says. "Now let's go see what this auction is all about." He tells me. As he tries to usher me through the crowd he places his firm hand on my back and it almost instantly takes my breath away. I find my body captivated by his touch and I find myself disappointed when he lets go once we make it to the other side.

The next two hours we spend sitting through the auction and when it's over, Derek helps me put on my coat and we make our exit. As we are walking out, I can't help but notice how empty my hand feels without Derek holding it. It's as if he's reading my mind because he then takes my hand in his and it gives me a warm fuzzy feeling. What is wrong with me? It's like I've turned into some hopeless romantic… or a sex driven maniac. I hope whoever is watching us, feels that we are compatible, because I don't even recognize who I am right now. I guess we'll find out tomorrow.

Once we make it back to the agency, I drop Derek off at his car. We both sit there silently for a moment, and I'm not sure if he wants to say something or if he's waiting on me to say something. I'm not exactly sure what there is to say though. He finally goes to get out of the car and I panic because a small part of me doesn't want him to leave.

"Thanks again for having my back tonight." I blurt out. He stops and looks at me, "No problem, that's what partners are for." Derek says. Now I'm his partner, what happened to being his wife? I actually feel a twinge of hurt. This just serves as another reminder that this is just a mission. I nod, "See you tomorrow." I tell him. "See ya." He tells me and then gets out of the car.

As I'm driving home, I can't help but feel like an idiot. This is why I like working alone. Less drama and no one to get in my head. It's just so hard to read Derek. I have to give it to him though, he sure can play the act very well. He is so convincing and then he goes and says things like *partner* and it throws me off. Oh well, tomorrow we'll find out if we passed and then we can move forward with the mission. Once we get to Russia, there won't be any breaks in our act and I need to prepare myself mentally for the emotional rollercoaster I'll be on. I'm not going to be one of the *weak* agents that blur the line of what's real and what's pretend. Some agents have to go to counseling when this happens and I don't want to be just another agent that can't handle accepting the truth that all the words and emotions expressed during a mission were an act. There's already the stigma against most female agents. They say we take it much harder when the mission's over. I've already told myself I'll never be one of those suckers, so looks like I better get my shit together.

Chapter 7: Liam

I didn't want to end the night abruptly, but if I would've stayed in the car a second longer, I don't know how much longer I would've been able to control myself. Ever since my dream, I keep picturing the image of Emma's half naked body on top of me and it's making it really hard to focus on anything else. She has no idea what she's doing to me and I'm sure she doesn't even care. I barely even know this girl, yet I would do anything for her, like eating a nasty ass mushroom. Never in a million years did I think I would eat a mushroom, but when she looked up at me with her beautiful blue eyes and asked me to, I couldn't tell her no. I'd do it all over again too, if she asked me.

I was worried she would get upset with me for coming to her defense when that prick Zach approached her, but she seemed grateful. She's probably tired of tactless guys hitting on her. Now, I'm not saying I'm some prince charming, but a woman like Emma doesn't deserve some sleaze bag who won't respect her. I can't wait to have her all to myself in Russia. Maybe then she can see how a man should treat her.

The next morning I show up early to work. I'm eager to see if we passed so me and Emma can move on with the mission. I've already tried to see if Randall would let it slip, but he's adamant about letting Ron break the news when Emma gets here. It's another ten minutes before Emma shows up and meets us in the conference room.

"Great, now that we are all here I'll get started. You two have completed both the interrogation and compatibility portions of your last test. You both passed the interrogation portion with flying colors and after reviewing the notes from your compatibility trial we have decided that you two are ready to proceed with the mission." Ron tells us. This is great! Now we can work on getting out of here. I look over at Emma and she has a faint smile on her face but still looks so serious. "So, now all you have left to undergo is a co-tactical session that will take place in about an hour. Once you're finished you'll be released home to start packing. You two will fly out at 1500 tomorrow and should arrive in Moscow at approximately 0900 the following day. Do either of you have any questions?" I shake my head while Emma raises her hand. "Yes Emma?" Ron questions. "Will our tickets and reservations be sent to our alias's emails?" Emma asks. "Good question Emma. Yes. Going forward all your tickets, confirmation numbers, and reservations will be found under your alias's email. You should go ahead and assume your alias's identity once you leave here today." Randall tells us. We both nod to show our comprehension. Once they are finished, they give us our passports and dismiss us.

I go up to Emma to express my excitement. "Hey wifey! You ready for our honeymoon?" I ask her. "Yep." She replies dryly. "I bet you already got everything packed." I say, trying to get her talking. "Pretty much." Is all she says. What hell is her deal? She's being so distant, when she was just fine last night. "Well I guess I'm gonna go ahead and get changed for our session." I tell her. "Okay." She says almost as if I'm annoying her.

I head to the locker room as I try to think of why she is being so short with me. I felt like yesterday went really good, but I guess not. After I get changed I wander over to the gym to do some warm up cardio. I run for about thirty minutes before heading over to the training room. I meet up with Emma again as they give us the scene for the scenario we are about to partake in. Unlike the first time me and Emma met, we are paired together. It's another one of the GACF's tests to see how well we work together.

Once we are ready, we take our place behind an empty crate and wait for the simulation to begin. From the chatter I've heard, Emma is one hell of an agent so I've been dying to see her action. When I hear the slight squeak of a door, I direct my attention in the direction of the sound. I can tell Emma heard it too, because she's scanning the field in the same direction. I'm about to motion for us to move forward when Emma takes off in the opposite direction. I decide to follow her and when I catch up to her she motions for me to stay back while she advances. Before I can tell her to let me advance instead, she leaves me behind. I focus back on the vast open area to the left of me and try to determine what I should do. After about five minutes I finally pick up on some foot steps that are approaching to my right. The steps sound too heavy for it to be Emma so I take a hiding place behind a wall to my left and hunker down. From my hiding place I pull out my scope and I can see one of the targets approaching where I just was. If I take my shot from here I'll give away my location, so I decide to wait until I can figure out where the others are. I watch my target advance further to the other side so I stealthily advance with him. Since I haven't seen any of his teammates tailing him, I'm hoping to corner him and then work my way back up. When we both make it to the end of the perimeter I pop up and take my shot. I hear the ding so I know I got him. I don't have much time to find cover so I make a run for a half wall nearby. I know my location is exposed when I hear shots fired in my direction as I slide into coverage. Shit. I know it's only a matter of time before I'm cornered, unless I make a ballsy move. I jump back up and shoot in the direction I heard the shots. The target shoots back and now I have his location. I wait a couple seconds to catch my breath. On the count of ten I pop up and expose myself, but I already have my aim locked on my targets location. I wait for my target to come up and as soon as he does I take my shot. A split second later I feel a kick to the back of one of my knees causing my legs to buckle and making me fall to my knees. Simultaneously, I hear a shot come from my right and another shot from behind me. I turn and look up to see Emma with her gun aimed to our right. I quickly look to my right and see a third target that would have got me if Emma didn't take me down. I didn't even see him.

"Thanks for the cover." I tell Emma, amazed by her stealthy surprise attack. "No problem, partner." Emma says, emphasizing the word partner hostilely. Now it clicks. Could she be upset that I referred to her as my partner last night? I didn't think that would come off so harsh, I just had to reduce the tension I was feeling. This must mean she actually likes pretending to be my wife. Could she possibly be feeling what I'm feeling too? There's no way to find out unless I just ask her, but I don't want to jeopardize the mission if she doesn't. Now the question is, how do I show her I didn't mean it that way without being too forward?

I stand up and dust myself off. "I am one lucky bastard to have you as my partner." I tell her. She cocks an eyebrow at me. "You are one hell of an agent and I can easily say I trust you with my life." I see her lips struggle to keep a smile from forming. "Thank you." She says. "Are you going to be ready for me to be your husband, full force starting tomorrow?" I ask her. "Why wouldn't I be?" She tells me. "Because, I've been holding back." I tell her racily followed by a wink. I see her let out a silent gasp and I flash her a pearly half smile. We hand in our guns and part our ways to the locker rooms.

Chapter 8: Stella

Oh my, I can't help but feel flush all over after Derek's comment. When I make it to the locker room to shower and change, I still have goosebumps lingering on me. So, maybe his calling me partner wasn't intentional. I find myself getting easily frustrated with how confused I am feeling. It shouldn't matter anyway. Once I finish getting dressed, I try to sneak out and head to the parking garage.

"Hey Em!" I hear Derek shout. I let out a small sigh and swivel around, "Hello Derek." "Already heading out?" He asks. "Yeah, I still have a few more things to pack before tomorrow." "Ah, okay. Well should we meet here and catch a ride to the airport?" Derek asks. "Sure, that sounds good. See you tomorrow." I tell him and walk off. It's not like I'm trying to avoid him, I just need to mentally prepare myself for what the next six months are going to hold.

When I make it home, I have some alone time since Kat doesn't get off for another two hours. Ever since I've told her about Derek she keeps teasing me about him, so it's nice to have some peace and quiet. I spend the next hour packing some last minute items and set my luggage by the door. Typically I'm bouncing off the walls with excitement and eager to go. Which I still am, but I also feel slightly nervous. I usually don't get pre-mission jitters, but for some reason I'm feeling anxious about this mission. It has to be because there is another factor involved, Derek.

I try to distract myself by laying down and reading a book to brush up on my Russian. It's been a couple years since I've had to speak or comprehend it. Even though our alias's are as American's, it's an advantage on our part to be able to understand what they are saying when they think we can't understand them. I wonder if Derek can speak Russian? I surely hope so since he will be the one around Chubinsky and his guys the most.

The next morning I say my goodbye to Kat and head out with my bags. When I make it to the agency, Derek is already in the main lobby waiting for me. When he spots me a big grin spreads across his face as he waves me over. As I approach him I can finally read his shirt that says *Hubby* in a fancy font. "Nice shirt." I say as I let out a chuckle. "Thanks!" He says proudly before continuing, "I actually got you a matching one." Derek tells me. He pulls a shirt from his bag that reads *Wifey* in the same fancy font and holds it out for me. I take the shirt from him, "You want me to wear this?" I ask. "Well yeah, we are supposed to be on our honeymoon after all. Don't you want to proudly show off our newly established marriage?" He says almost convincingly. I let out a laugh, "I guess so. Let me go change shirts real quick." I tell him.

After I emerge from the bathroom, me and Derek do a last minute run through to make sure we have all of our documents. Once we make sure everything is accounted for we fetch a taxi to make our journey to the airport. As soon as we get in the car the taxi driver turns around looks at us, "Honeymoon huh?" The man asks. "Yep." Derek says as he puts his arm around me and nuzzles his face into my neck." I let out a giggle as his stubble tickles me. "Well aren't y'all adorable." The driver says while flashing us a smile, "To the airport I'm guessing?" "You got it." Derek tells him. Derek keeps his arm around me for the duration of the ride and I play my part by leaning into him.

When we make it to the airport, we pay the man and collect our bags. We then proceed to check in and go through TSA. We don't have much time to spare once we make it through TSA so we head straight to our terminal and wait to board the plane. Oddly enough, it's spare time like this that makes the job difficult. Since we aren't allowed to talk about our true identities, it limits our discussion material and we already know everything about the alias's identities so the conversation is redundant. If we don't talk though, it makes us look suspicious, especially as newly weds.

As we board the plane, a few of the people let out a chorus of *awe's* as we pass them. Derek lets me have the window seat while he takes the middle and as we are waiting for the other passengers to take their seats, we pick out a movie to watch. A few moments later, a middle aged gentleman takes his spot in the aisle seat in our row. Once the man settles in his seat he nudges Derek to get his attention. "Goin' on the honeymoon I see." The man says in a heavy country accent. "We sure are." Derek says excitedly while I offer a big smile. The man lets out a chuckle, "Well I'd hate to have the room next to yours." He says. I immediately blush as Derek lets out a chuckle in return. "If we can keep our hands off each other that long. Isn't that right babe?" Derek replies as he plants a kiss on my cheek. I let out a giggle, "Mhm." I say as I sensually run my fingers through Derek's hair. It's apparent we've made the man uncomfortable as he lets out an awkward chuckle and then pulls out a book to read. Derek glances at me and we exchange a silent laugh.

The rest of the flight is uneventful and we make our connecting flight with no issues. By time we board the second flight that will be flying us into Moscow, I am exhausted. I try to fight the sleep, but my body finally succumbs to the exhaustion and I end up falling asleep. It's not till we land that I wake up. I blink a couple times till my eyes adjust to the still dark cabin and then I realize my head is resting on Derek's shoulder and his head is resting on mine. I nudge him awake and he offers a big yawn and stretches out his arms.

"Man that was a good nap." Derek comments. "Yes, much needed." I reply. "We just landed." I add as I open the window, letting in the morning light. Derek lets out a groan, "You could've warned a person." "Sorry. I'm an early bird so you better get use to me waking you up early." I joke. "And I'm a night owl, so, you better get use to me keeping you up late." Derek teases back with a wink. I can feel my face get warm. "Ugh, get a room." The woman in our row scoffs. We both let out a small laugh.

Once we get off the plane, we make a bathroom stop and then head to the baggage claim. After we get our bags we fetch our rental car and Derek drives us to the hotel. I enjoy our ride, which is no surprise. Russia is a beautiful country, with so many things to see. I was excited to be coming back. We are staying at a different hotel than I have previously, but this one is pretty snazzy so I can't complain. I check in and get our keys while Derek loads up the cart with our luggage. We then make our way to our room. "Wait!" Derek says before I open the door. "What is it?" I ask cautiously, incase he picked up on something I may not have noticed. "Allow me." Derek says as he swiftly swoops me off my feet and carries me through the threshold. "You are crazy." I tell him. "Only for you." He says as he sets me down. We stare intensely at each other for a few seconds until I turn away to admire the room. "This is a nice place." I say as I walk around. "Heck yeah!" I hear Derek exclaim from the other room. As I round the corner I see Derek plopping down on the large king sized bed in the middle of the room. "This bed is so comfortable." He comments as he closes his eyes. "What are you doing?" I ask rhetorically. "I'm taking a nap." He says. "We have to unpack our stuff." I tell him. "Yeah, but we don't have to do it right this second." He murmurs. I let out a huff, but he doesn't budge.

Eager to get settled in as soon as possible, I head back to the main room to unpack our things. I also take it upon myself to put our passports and important documents in the safe. Once I'm done I take a quick shower and change into some fresh clothes. Derek is still asleep and as much as I want to sleep as well, I am nervous to join him on the bed. Obviously we would have to share a bed, I just hadn't given it much thought till now. Instead I make myself comfy on the couch and find myself dozing off.

When I finally wake up, I find myself in the bed. I don't remember waking up and getting into the bed, so that means Derek must have carried me to bed. I smile at the sweet gesture, but then remind myself he must have felt bad that I ended up sleeping on the couch while he was in the bed. I stretch my body and then get out bed. I take in a deep inhale and detect the smell of food. He better not have went and got food without me, I think to myself. I follow the delicious aroma and find Derek in the kitchenette making some food. I stand there for a moment as I admire his physique and watch his movements as he cooks.

"Hello sleepy head." Derek says when he notices my appearance. "Hi." I say bashfully. "Hungry?" He asks. "I'm starving." I reply. "Good, it's about time to eat." He states. "What time is it anyway?" I ask as I look for a clock. "It's almost five." "Your kidding." I say shocked. He lets out a chuckle, "Nope. I think we were more jet lagged than we thought." "I guess so." I say. Now I'm not going to be able to sleep tonight, I think to myself. "Sit." Derek commands as he motions toward our table. I take my seat as Derek brings me a plate and places it in front of me. "Is this chicken Alfredo?" I ask. "Sure is." He replies proudly. I give him a smirk, "I thought I was supposed be the one that cooks?" "I thought I'd give you the first night off since you'll be doing it for the next six months." He replies. I roll my eyes, "Oh joy." I reply. "Plus, it's my way of thanking you for putting away all my stuff." Derek says. "No problem. After all it gave me dibs on where to put my stuff." I tell him. "See, about time I get credit for taking a nap. I would be glad to do so anytime." Derek tells me. "I'm sure." I say letting out a laugh.

Once we finish dinner, I wash the dishes while Derek dries and puts them away. We then retreat to the couch to watch some TV and sit in silence for about an hour until Derek rises from his seat. "I think I'm gonna go down to the gym for a bit." "Oh, okay." I reply, as I watch him go into the room and shortly re-emerge in some gym clothes. Now I have the urge to go to the gym, but decide against it so he doesn't think I'm just keeping an eye on him.

I turn off the TV while I ponder over the plan for tomorrow. We received word that some of Viktor's guys will be hanging around one of the markets in Moscow so our first objective will be to see if we can witness any deals take place. I'm hoping we are able to gain some beneficial intel during this outing. If we can get the name of one of the companies they work with, then Derek will have an idea of which companies to pitch his proposals too. Now feeling a little more at ease, I decide to call it a night. If I go to bed first then maybe I won't feel so awkward when Derek comes to bed.

I'm not sure how long I had been asleep, but when I hear the door, I sit straight up. "Derek?" I call aloud. There's no response and my mind starts to imagine the worst. I quietly get out of bed and crouch beside the bedroom door. As soon as the lights flick on I spring out from my hiding spot and deliver a punch to the chest of my now identified intruder. He grabs my opposite wrist to keep me from delivering another punch. "What the hell Emma?" Derek says as he tries to catch his breath. "I'm sorry, I called your name and you didn't answer so I thought you were someone breaking in." "I had my headphones in, geez." He says as he rubs his chest. "Sorry." I mumble once more. "It's fine. I didn't mean to startle you." He says. Unsure of what to say, I go to get back in bed and make myself comfortable. Derek keeps his eyes on me as he takes his shirt off and tosses it in the laundry bin. I try my best to not let his shirtless presence affect me, but holy shit. He's even sexier than I imagined. The sweat he's accumulated accentuates his muscular physique and his nearly developed six pack. Once I catch my eyes trailing down towards his v-line I quickly meet his eyes once again. "Um, what are you doing?" I ask hastily, trying to pretend as if I'm not enjoying the view. "Taking a shower or I could just come straight to bed if that's what you prefer?" He tells me with a smirk. "No, I'd prefer if you didn't come to bed smelling like ass." I tell him. He lets out a laugh and it helps ease some of the tension I am feeling. I turn away from him and pull the cover up to my neck to signal my end of the conversation. I hear Derek go into the bathroom and turn on the shower. My mind starts to wander as I picture Derek in the shower and what would happen if I were to join him. I shake my head to get the image out of my thoughts. I don't need to be thinking this way.

After twenty minutes pass, Derek is finished with his shower and I do my best to pretend as if I'm asleep so I don't have to make anymore small talk. As Derek gets in the bed, the manly aroma of his body wash follows him and it makes me want to take a deep inhale. Despite having a king sized bed, Derek cozies his body up to mine and puts his arm around me. I can tell he doesn't have a shirt on and I can only wonder if he has shorts on. I try to maintain my composure when the touch of his hand grazes my leg.

"Goodnight." He whispers in my ear and causes every hair on my body to stand. Surprisingly, it doesn't take me long to fall asleep. Derek's warmth and comforting embrace puts me quickly to sleep.

Chapter 9: Liam

The next morning I wake up, feeling more refreshed than I have in a long time. I look down and I see Emma's head resting on my chest and her leg overlapping mine. Talk about a bad time to have to piss because I want to savor this moment. I watch the gentle rise and fall of her breathing while I use my freehand to brush the hair out of her face. I admire her face and luscious lips and catch myself wanting to kiss her. My thoughts quickly turn x-rated and now I find myself pitching a tent.

Another couple minutes pass until Emma starts to shift. I close my eyes so she doesn't think I'm some creep watching her sleep. She lets out a small gasp and quickly pulls herself off of me. I pretend to wake up once she rolls away. "Everything okay?" I ask groggily. "Yes, I just, um wanted to be up by now." She says. She gets out of bed and opens the window shade. As the bright light shines through I let out a groan. "Why?" I ask rhetorically. "Because isn't the sunlight just beautiful?" She asks jokingly as she basks in the light. I watch her soak in the sun and I become mesmerized by how beautiful she looks, "It sure is." I tell her.

She goes over to the dresser and pulls out some clothes and then goes into the bathroom. I guess that's my cue to get out of bed and get dressed. We got a big day ahead and I'm hoping we have some luck with getting the info we need. I throw on some nice jeans and a polo. You don't want to stand out but you also don't want to blend in too much. It's a very stressful ordeal. "Hey Em, where's my belt?" I ask through the bathroom door. She opens the door while she's brushing her teeth and walks over to the closet and pulls it from a drawer. "Thanks babe, you're the best." I tell her. She rolls her eyes at me before returning to the bathroom. I finish getting ready and then head into the kitchen to see what I can eat for breakfast.

As I'm munching on some cereal, Emma emerges from the bedroom. "Well you look nice." I tell her. She offers a small smile and then swiftly goes into the kitchen. I'm not sure why she gets so embarrassed with my compliments, you'd think she would be aware of how gorgeous she is. Then I suddenly remember that she said she's never had a boyfriend before. She must be use to all the slimy horn dogs pawning after one thing. Just the thought of some asshole trying to take advantage of Emma has my primal instincts clawing their way to the surface. I have the urge to claim her as mine and protect her at all costs. I hate feeling this way, because I've never concerned myself with other people, especially their feelings. Growing up I was taught not to trust anyone who Ma and Pa didn't know and I think that's why I've always been so guarded mentally and emotionally. Yet here I am, willing to do whatever this captivating woman in front of me asks. Hell, I'm already trying my hardest to make her happy the best I can. After all, the last thing I wanted was this sugary cereal, but there was only one yogurt and I know that yogurt is one of her favorite breakfast items. As I see her face light up as she pulls the yogurt from the fridge, I realize the frozen the walls around my heart are starting to crumble.

Of course Emma suggests to walk so we can take in the scenery, but I don't mind. That means just more one on one time with her. I grab my jacket and we make our way to the market. As we walk I take the opportunity to hold her hand. I hope it doesn't make her uncomfortable, I just want to be close to her. When we make it to the market, we browse through the shops. I can tell Emma is really tense and I know it's because she is so goal oriented and we have a big surface to cover. It doesn't help we don't know who we are looking for. As much as it pains me to put Emma at risk, I think of a plan that will most likely work.

I pull her up against me and I can tell she is confused, but goes along with it. I intend to give her a quick kiss, but I can't help myself and we exchange a long kiss. "What are you doing?" She whispers as she kisses my neck. Her soft lips on my neck, stun me for a moment. "I have a plan to draw out the guys." I tell her as I now kiss along her neck. She giggles as she lets out an "Mhm." "Let's split up. Scumbags always approach a pretty girl by herself." I whisper as I nuzzle my face in her neck. She pulls away from me and gives me an exaggerated pouty face. "Babe can I please go look at the other shops while you go deal with work." She says out loud. This time I opt for a quick kiss on her pouted lips. "Fine, but meet me back here in an hour." I tell her. Damn, she deserves an Oscar I think to myself.

As she walks off into the crowd, I can't help but feel anxious. It makes me nervous sending her off on her own like that, but she hasn't had a partner up till now and besides, she's perfectly capable of handling her own. I go look at a couple nearby shops and then take my place outside the cafe where me and Emma parted ways. I order us both a coffee as she should be returning soon. When it's five minutes past when we agreed to meet, I start to worry and pull out my phone to call her. All of a sudden I hear Emma's laugh from behind me. As I look over my shoulder, Emma has her arm looped around some man. I clench my jaw, to keep me from speaking my mind, as this guy must be of use to us.

I rise from my chair and give Emma a harsh look and she quickly unlinks arms with the man. "Did you forget whose wife you are sweetie?" I tell her. "Of course not." She says skittishly and then takes her place beside me. The man sticks out his hand for me to shake. "I am Mikhail. Your wife has told me about your interest in building a foreign trade branch while you are here." He says in a thick Russian accent. "Indeed I am." I tell him. "The man I work for might be interested in helping with your success here in Russia." Mikhail says and then cautiously glances at Emma. I pull out my wallet, "It looks like your gallivanting about has been of use my love. Why don't you go buy something pretty for later while the men talk business." I tell her. She gives me a smile and takes the money, but as she goes to walk off I pull her back into a kiss before releasing her. I look into her eyes, "Don't be late again." I tell her firmly as I hand her, the coffee.

Once Emma disappears, Mikhail joins me at the table. "How serious are you about getting this branch going?" Mikhail asks. "This will be my second expansion, and if it's as successful as my first, then all parties involved will have the potential to be, let's just say, very happy." I tell him. He just nods. "I automatically provide sixty percent. I have an investor willing to submit twenty percent if I could just find one more investor willing to pick up the remaining twenty. Then I'd be able to submit the proposal to get things started." "Very well. My boss might be interested. I'll pass along the numbers and see what he says. Give me your number and I'll contact you if he's interested." I write my number down and hand it to him. As he goes to grab it I hold onto it and look him directly in the eyes. "Our visa's are only good for six months, so don't bullshit around." I tell him gruffly. He gives me a smug look as I finally let him take the paper.

I sit back in my seat and let out a large huff. I guess that didn't go too bad. I feel like I seemed pretty convincing. I start to look around for Emma. I'd really like to just get back to the hotel and decompress. I feel someone grab my shoulder and I quickly turn around to see Emma standing behind me. "Gotcha." She says teasingly. I pull her around and onto to my lap and hug her tight. Despite how stressed I am, her presence alone eases me. She rubs her fingers through my hair and I have to admit when Anna does it, I find it annoying, but when Emma does it, I find it soothing. "Did you find anything you like?" I ask her. "Not really. But I probably should have bought some other shoes because my feet are killing me from walking around so much." She says as her brows furrow. "Alright, fine." I tell her as I stand while cradling her in my arms. "What are you doing?" Emma asks. "Well since your feet hurt, I'm going to carry you back to the hotel." "Derek that's over a mile and a half." She tells me before adding, "I feel so silly. You're carrying me like a baby." "Well you should have thought about that beforehand." She flashes me her dazzling smile, "You put me down Derek Matthews." "Fine, will you settle for a piggy back ride?" I ask her. She thinks about it for a second before responding. "If you insist and only cause my feet really do hurt." She tells me. I set her down and I kneel down as she hops on my back. She starts to laugh as I stand up and start to walk. "I have to say, I've never had a piggy back ride. This is pretty amusing." Emma says. I let out a chuckle, "Your dad never gave you one growing up?" I ask. "I never knew my…" her voice trails off, and I can tell for a split second she forgot who and where she was. "I never knew my dad in that sense, is what I meant. He was always too busy with work. He didn't have much time for silly things like piggy back rides." She says followed by a nervous chuckle. I can tell the mishap makes her uncomfortable so I change the subject. "So, what do you plan on making for dinner?" I ask. I'm not sure yet, I haven't had a chance to look over the cabinets yet." "I'm sure it'll be great regardless." I tell her.

When we finally make it back to the hotel, I set her down and she gives me a soft shy smile. "My feet thank you tremendously." Emma tells me. "Anytime." I tell her as I brush the hair out of her face. As eager as I am to be in the comfort of our room, I enjoy being in public because I can be closer with Emma without it seeming weird. As much as I want to kiss her right now, I opt for holding her hand.

Chapter 10: Stella

When we make it back to the room, I'm still in disbelief that I almost slipped up on my cover. I knew this would be a problem. I just find it so easy to talk with Derek that sometimes I catch myself wanting to be the real me. Despite my screw up, I am still overly pleased with our success today. It was pure luck that I came across Mikhail in the market, he is one of the men in Viktor's immediate circle. This means our mission is potentially ahead of schedule as long as we can can get Viktor to take our bait.

I must admit it was a clever plan on Derek's part for us to split up. One thing that never fails to get a guys attention is a confused female all by herself who is clueless about something. All it takes is a low cut shirt and acting like you don't know what something is and voila. I can only imagine how Derek would've reacted if he would've seen Mikhail come onto me. As I was loudly expressing my confusion over a transaction at one of the stands, Mikhail came behind me and quite literally pulled me aside to help explain it for me. With his hand lingering on my ass, I did my best to maintain my helpless tourist demeanor. I thanked him dramatically for his help and then explained how my husband has been too busy working on his new foreigns trade business to come shopping with me. Of course this peaked Mikhail's interest as he tried to ask me more questions, but being the good clueless spoiled house wife I am, I told Mikhail that I'm not sure what Derek does. All I know is he is always talking about numbers and different people and places and he makes good money for it and that's all that matters. I then asked if he would walk me back to meet Derek because I felt unsafe being a female alone in a foreign country and all. It all seemed to fall into place perfectly.

While I'm attempting to make dinner, I reminisce on the kisses we exchanged before we split up. I rub my hand where he kissed along my neck and the memory alone gives me goosebumps. It took every ounce of will power for me to stop. I remember walking away and feeling so sexually frustrated that I was in a daze for about ten minutes, trying to process it all.

The smell of burning vegetables brings me back to reality. "Shit." I say aloud. I've never been that great of a cook. I can make a couple meals, but Kat is usually the one who cooks. I quickly move the skillet off the burner and grimace as I look over the mostly burnt vegetables. Kat gave me a few recipes in hopes of impressing *the good kisser* with my cooking abilities. So much for that I think as I scoff to myself. At least the meat for the stir fry is okay.

"Everything okay in here?" Derek says as he comes into the kitchen. "Um. We might have a slight problem." I say as I let the embarrassment fall across my face. He peers into the skillet and sees the charred vegetables. "Extra crispy. Just the way I like them." He tells me jokingly. I reply with a bashful grin. "Anything I can do to help?" He asks. "It's just about done, if you wanna get out the plates and silverware." I tell him.

I can't help but notice that neither of us finish our plate of food and it makes me feel like the worst cook ever. He ate more of it than I did and claimed he was full. I don't blame him, for not eating it all though. I clean up the mess and then go the gym. I've been itching to release the built up tension and endorphins I've accumulated over the past few days. I choose to do a five mile run on the treadmill and it's the perfect stress reliever. I work up a pretty good sweat and when I'm finished I feel so much better. I can't wait to get back to the room and take a nice warm shower to top off my workout. When I get back to the room, Derek isn't in the main room so I make my way into the bedroom.

"Oh!" I say as I quickly turn around. It would be my luck, I walk in on Derek in nothing but a towel. "What's wrong?" Derek asks. "Sorry, I should've announced myself." I tell him. I hear his steps grow closer until I feel him stop behind me. "Why? I'm your husband." He says in a husky tone and his warm breath travels down my neck. I suddenly crave his lips on my neck where they were earlier. With my heart pounding and every part of me telling me not to, I turn around to face him. I slowly take in his bare chiseled chest and sculpted biceps and when my eyes finally meet his, my knees buckle and he steadies me. "Careful." He whispers. I can feel my face become flush from his naked proximity, and the thoughts that I'm having to go along with it aren't helping. I clear my throat, "If you'll excuse me I need to shower." His stare lingers for a moment before he steps aside and lets me pass. I quickly make my way to the bathroom and shut the door.

I let out a large huff as I ponder over what just happened. I've never been so distracted by another person's presence like this, what is going on with me? Not too mention his stare was so intense, I felt more vulnerable the longer I looked into his eyes. This is uncharted territory for me and I don't like this feeling. I'm use to being independent and having sloppy hook ups, but when I'm with Derek I have this burning desire to share everything with him and make him happy. It's like no one or nothing else matters. Maybe my hormones are just raging because of the lack of intimacy I've had lately. I can hear Kat's teasing words, *he's so got you all hot and bothered.* As of right now, she wouldn't be wrong, I think to myself. I try to brush off my embarrassment and take my shower in peace.

When I'm finished, I turn off the water and go to get out of the shower when I realize I forgot my towel. I clench my fists in frustration, how could I be such an idiot. This could not happen at an even worse time. I let out a large sigh and try to maintain my dignity as I call out for Derek. "Derek." I say as I put my ear to the door. I don't hear him respond. "Derek!" I shout. This time I hear some commotion, then a light knock on the door. "Emma, everything okay?" Derek asks. "Could you... grab me a towel?" I ask reluctantly. I hear him walk off and then return. "Here you go." He tells me. I barely crack the door to try and retrieve the towel. "I think you're gonna have to open it more than that." Derek tells me. I open the door a bit more and now I can see the smug look on his face as he holds out a towel. I snatch it from him and quickly shut the door, but then realize I don't have any clean clothes either. "You can go away now!" I shout. "Or you can just come on out? I won't mind." Derek says teasingly. Realizing I don't really have a choice I wrap the towel around me and emerge from the bathroom.

I open the door ready to reply with a snarky comment, but when I do he's gone and the bedroom door is shut. I catch myself grinning at his subtle sign on respect. I make my way over to the dresser and get changed into my pajamas. Once I'm finished, I open the door and see Derek sitting on the couch. I perch myself in the doorway and to my viewing pleasure, Derek still doesn't have a shirt on and is just wearing a pair of shorts. "I'm done." I tell him. He stands up and stretches, which emphasizes his biceps. "Good, 'cause I think it's time we call it a night." Derek says, as he makes his way towards me. "Um, excuse me? Surely, you aren't speaking for me." I say a bit shocked. He stops in front of me, "It was more of a suggestion." He says as he picks me up and throws me over his shoulder. "Hey, what are you doing? Put me down." I tell him. "As you wish." He says as drops me onto the bed. I let out a laugh as I hit the bed, but then my focus is quickly directed on Derek towering over me. Our eyes are locked as he climbs onto the bed and as he hovers over me I hold my breath. "Goodnight Emma." Derek whispers and then rolls over to his side of the bed. I finally let out a breath and turn to face the opposite way. "Goodnight." I murmur.

I don't know what game he is playing, but whatever it is, he's good at it. Does he think if he seduces me, but I'm the one who makes the move then he can't be at fault? Well two can play at that game. Not that anything is going to happen between us, but *if* it were to happen, he'd be the one

making a move first. Listen to me, I sound pathetic.
Contemplating the possibility of sleeping with my partner, is
not like me at all. This is all just a cover I tell myself sternly,
none of his feelings or words mean anything. Coincidentally,
Derek drapes his arm over me and pulls me into a cuddle and
it's as if everything I just tried to reassure myself seems to
fade away.

Chapter 11: Liam

It's been five days since I spoke with Mikhail and I am starting to get nervous. Maybe he didn't take the bait after all. I can't let my nerves get the best of me, we knew this would take time, I just have to be patient. In the meantime I've moved forward with establishing a vacant office space and applying for the permits. If that doesn't get the word around town about how serious I am then I don't know what will. Emma's been really good at reassuring me that this is going to work. I always seem to think of the worst on missions, so Emma being here helps keep my pessimist attitude at bay.

I hate to admit it, but I've been short with Emma the past few days. Partly because I've been stressed about the mission, but also because I'm growing dangerously attracted to Emma and I don't want to ruin things between us. Today we are going out to dinner since we've been cooped up the last few days and I think it'll do us good. I also want to give her a break from cooking. I know she's trying her best, but it's evident cooking is not one of her strong suits and I hate seeing her feel ashamed over something so silly.

"I'm almost ready." Emma shouts from the bathroom. I can hear a bunch of her makeup clinking around. "Okay. No worries." I've never seen her so frazzled, but me telling her I was taking her on a date tonight seemed to throw her off guard. As she emerges from the bathroom, I see she has a little more makeup on than usual and is wearing a nice blouse with a pencil skirt that hugs her sexy coke bottle figure. "You look great." I tell her. She offers me a soft smile, "Thank you. You don't look so bad yourself." She replies.

When we make it to the restaurant, the waiter leads us to our table and I take it upon myself to pull out Emma's chair. Even though I don't want to cross the line with Emma, she also deserves to know how a man should treat her. Once we order, we are left staring at one another. "So, are you enjoying our honeymoon so far?" I ask. "Of course. I just wish you didn't have to work so much." She tells me with a frown. I raise an eyebrow, "Why's that?" "Think of how much more fun we could have." She tells me, as she rubs her foot up my leg. I lean forward to help ease my brewing sexual tension. "Well, I think I can work something out." I tell her. She leans forward, leaving our faces inches apart. "Oh we can work something out alright." She tells me seductively.

Hot damn, what's gotten into her? The last time Emma came on to me was in a dream, but I know for a fact I'm awake. Her luscious lips are barely inches apart from mine and I can smell the sweet aroma of her perfume. It's taking every bit of restraint not to kiss her right now, but if she persists, I don't know if I'll be able to control myself. "Keep it up and we'll just skip dinner." I tell her with a smirk. She bites her bottom lip, "Is that a promise?" She says. I purse my lips, unsure of what to say and she sits back in her seat with a pleased look on her face. If she only knew how much of a rise out of me. I feel a hand on my shoulder and I look up to see Mikhail. I would think of him as a cock-block, but now it makes sense as to why Emma was acting the way she was. I should've known she wasn't interested in me that way.

"Why hello." I say to Mikhail. "Oh my gosh, Mikhail!" Emma says in an excited tone. Mikhail turns to Emma and gives her a big smile, "Hello Emma, good to see you again." Mikhail tells her before redirecting his attention back to me. "Your proposal has been accepted, except my boss wants to take on the whole forty percent. We'll be in touch." Mikhail says as he holds out his hand. I shake his hand and I feel him slide me a note. He turns back to Emma and takes her hand and kisses it, "Farewell for now." He tells her and offers me a parting nod. I nod back and he walks off.

I'm not sure if he has been following us or how long he has been watching us, but regardless our cover has worked. I swiftly tuck the paper in my pocket and direct my attention back to Emma. She offers me a soft smile as if to apologize for her previous actions and I offer a smile in return. Luckily the food comes out at this time so we don't have to make much small talk.

When we make it back to the hotel I'm anxious to show Emma the note. Once we enter the room I grab Emma by the wrist and put my index finger to my mouth to indicate her to be quiet. I retrieve the note from my pocket and hold it out for both of us to read.

Tomorrow 1000, at the market, alone.

We look at one another and exchange a big grin. Now that we got him to take the bait, we just have to get solid evidence. Then we can nail Chubinsky and some of his henchmen. I immediately retreat to the room to go over my proposal pitch and gather all the corresponding documents. It's not till I can't find one of the documents that I emerge from the room.

I see Emma sitting on the couch watching TV. I don't want to worry her so I head to the kitchen table and shuffle through the papers, but it's not there either. After looking through the papers for a third time I get frustrated and push the papers off the table. "Where the hell is the damn lease?" I say out-loud. I think Emma senses my stress and comes over to me. She bends down to pick up the papers and I stop her. "Don't. It's my mess, you shouldn't have to clean it up." "We're in this together." She tells me before continuing to help pick up the papers. "Here." She says as she pulls the document from the pile of papers she hands me. "Of course you'd find it." I tell her. She gives me a smile, "I think it's time to go to bed." She tells me. "I still don't even have my pitch down pact Em." "It was more of a suggestion." She tells me with a smirk. "Are you mocking me Mrs. Matthews?" She lets out a giggle and I can't help, but laugh too. "Fine, if you insist." I tell her. I set down the papers and go to grab her. "Oh no you don't." She says as she dodges my grasp and makes a run for the bedroom. I chase her into the room and gently tackle her onto the bed. Our eyes lock and as she looks up at me with her mesmerizing blue eyes I forget for a split moment that this is all just cover and I kiss her. Once I realize what I've done, I pull away and get up quickly. I clear my throat, "I'm sorry it's been a stressful day. I'm gonna shower and then I'll come to bed."

I'm such an idiot, I think to myself. Why would I do that? I can only imagine the post-op report she's going to file. As if I didn't have enough stress on my plate. I take my shower and then head to bed. At least Emma is asleep, or at least pretending to be save us from the awkwardness. I debate sleeping on the couch, but I don't want to draw more attention to the situation so I just go to bed.

The next morning I wake up and Emma is already out of bed. I let out a sigh. I get up and get dressed and as I enter the main room, I can smell breakfast. "Good morning. Breakfast is ready." She tells me cheerily. "Well thanks, you didn't have to do all this." "No worries, I wanted to." She says as she places a plate of eggs, toast and bacon in front of me. "Coffee or orange juice?" She asks. "Coffee." I tell her. I give her a puzzled expression as she hands me a cup of coffee. "What? Can't a wife cater to her husband?" "I just feel bad, I should be the one making you breakfast." I tell her shamefully. She sits on my lap and puts her arm around me. "It's okay." She whispers to me and then kisses my temple. As she goes to get up, I hold her tight and she looks at me. "Thank you." I tell her as I deliver a kiss to her forehead. She gives me a blushing smile and then gets up to make her plate.

Once I finish breakfast I gather all of the documents and get ready to leave. "Wait!" Emma says. I turn around and she approaches me prudently. She looks nervous, "What's wrong?" I ask her. "I just, um, wanted to wish you luck at your meeting." She tells me. "Oh, well thanks babe." I tell her. "And be safe. Remember, stranger danger." She tells me followed by a nervous chuckle and now it hits me. She's worried about me. I'd have to say if the situation was reversed, I'd be worried sick for her. I wouldn't be able to just sit back and let her go out by herself. I offer a warm smile and nod to show her I understand, "Of course babe, I'll be back soon."

I make it to the market with fifteen minutes to spare so I order a drink and take a seat. When they don't show up by 10:15 I know they are probably watching to see how I react and see if I try to contact someone, which would be a rookie mistake. I finish off my drink and slam it down and then gather my things in a frustrated manner and get ready to leave. "Waste of my damn time." I mutter. Almost instantly, I hear my name.

"Ah Derek, there you are." Mikhail says. I turn around to see Mikhail with some tall buff ex-military looking man that I have never seen before. "Hello Mikhail." "Our boss sends his apologies. He is running behind, but asked us to go ahead and get things started." Mikhail tells me. "Very well. I was starting to think I got stood up." I say in annoyed tone. "I'm sure the boss will make up for it when he gets here." I look at the man with Mikahil and look him up and down to prompt his introduction. He sticks out his hand, "I'm Dimitri." He says in a Russian accent. "Derek." I reply as I shake his hand. We take a seat and they order a round of drinks. I'm sure this is a part of their plan. Get me tipsy to increase my chances of slipping up.

After our second round of drinks, Dimitri gets a call. "I'll be back." He says and leaves me and Mikhail alone. I try to make small talk so I appear more personal. "Hey man can you help me out with something?" Mikhail raises a brow. "Know any fancy places I can take the wife? She's been itching to go out since we got here, but I haven't had the time." He lets out a chuckle, "I think I might have an idea, but I'll have to clear it with the boss first." I give a nod. "Please tell me once we become partners, I don't have to call him *the boss*. That might just be a deal breaker." I say. Mikhail just stares at me for a second, but then lets out a laugh. "Funny guy. No, you aren't that special." Mikhail says. "Now look whose the comedian." We both let out a chuckle.

I see Mikhail's face turn serious as he stands up and nods. I turn around and rise up from my chair as I see Dimitri approaching us with a short plump man, who I recognize as the one and only, Viktor Chubinsky. I stick out my hand, "You must be the boss. I'm Derek Matthews." I say. He shakes my hand, "Viktor. Sorry for the delay, there was some business that needed tending to." He says in a heavy Russian accent. "Shall we?" I say motioning to the table. We all take our seats and then Viktor orders us another round of drinks as I start my pitch.

After thirty minutes and two more rounds of drinks we are all laughing and discussing different business tactics. It's not till Chubinsky gets a call that the fun stops. He keeps his conversation short and discrete. "No. Get it done." He says to the person on the phone. Once he ends the call, he directs his attention on me. "Show me where I need to sign." He tells me. "Really?" I ask. He just gives me a nod. I pull out the documents and he signs each of them. "Mikhail and

Dimitri will be helping me handle our arrangements. There's no going back on our deal and if you try to screw me over it won't end well for you, or your wife." Viktor tells me. Although I know he is a mafia leader, his forwardness so soon catches me off guard. "Excuse me?" I say. He scoffs at me, "You have no idea who you're doing business with. Just stay on my good side and you'll be just fine. If I find out you tried to cross me I'll let my men have their way with your wife while you're forced to watch, and then I'll kill you." "You sick bastard." I say through clenched teeth. He lets out sadistic chuckle. "A deals a deal Mr. Matthews. Like I said, just stay on my good side." He then sticks out his hand to solidify the deal. I hesitate so I appear reluctant and afraid, and then shake his hand. I snatch my papers back from him and put them away. "Pleasure doing business with you." He says as he rises from his chair. "Yeah, yeah. When are you gonna transfer me the money?" I tell him. "Mikhail will get your banking details and it should be there by tonight." "It better be." I tell him. Dimitri puffs out his chest in defense of Viktor. "You wanna go big boy?" I say as I set down my briefcase. "It's alright Dimitri. Derek here has the right priorities. Money is the main objective here." Viktor says as he pats us both on the shoulder. "Damn straight, so stay out of my way and let me do my job so I can make us both happy." I tell him. "Likewise." Chubinsky says and then leaves with Dimitri following him.

"I can't believe you work for that prick." I tell Mikhail. Mikhail remains silent and looks away ashamed. "Anyways, here's what you need for the account." I say as I write down the bank info and give it to Mikhail. I give him the paper and we both part our ways.

As I make my way back to the hotel, I can't wait to hit the gym. I can't believe Viktor had the audacity to threaten Emma like that. The thought of his nasty henchmen defiling Emma has me seeing red. It took everything I had not to kill him right then and there, even if it meant I'd lose my job.

When I make it back to the room, Emma greets me with a look of relief. "How'd it go?" She asks. I ignore her question and pull her into a long hug. "I promise I will never let anything happen to you." She pulls away and gives me horrified look. "What are you talking about?" She asks. "Nothing, I just wanted to make that clear. The meeting went good, Mikhail's boss signed the papers so everything is set to start. I should have the money by tonight." She signs to me, *Chubinsky*? I give her a nod. "Wow babe that's great, I am so happy for you. I told you it would all work out." She tells me.

Chapter 12: Stella

It's been three days since Derek went to meet with Viktor and his men, and he has been overly cautious since then. I don't know if it's his nerves or what, but he hasn't been himself. I'd be lying if I said I didn't' miss his usual banter and overly friendly demeanor. It's also killing me to just sit back and be practically useless. We can't even discuss the mission or any evidence he has gathered without potential risks. Especially now that we have made contact with Viktor, there's a great chance that he may have had our room bugged. This is were it becomes critical to stay alert and on point so we don't compromise our cover.

"Babe, can you come here?" I hear Derek ask from the main room. "Just a second, I'm just finishing up." I throw on a shirt and make my way into the room and I see Mikhail standing in the doorway. "Babe, you didn't tell me we were gonna be having company, I would've made lunch." I tell Derek. "Pardon the intrusion Emma, I was just coming by to extend an invitation to a party tonight." Mikhail says. "A party?" I say excitedly, as I clasp my hands together. Mikhail lets out a laugh, "Your husbands new business partner throws an annual black tie ball to get all of his investors and partners together. You two are on the list and Viktor hopes to see you two there." Mikhail replies. "A ball!" I squeal. "I didn't pack for this. Babe we need to go get me a dress!" Derek and Mikhail laugh. "What time?" Derek asks. "Seven." "We'll be there." Derek says as he shakes Mikhail's hand. "I'll let him know. Goodbye Emma." Mikhail says as he offers a parting wave. "See you later Mikhail. Thanks for the invite." I reply.

Derek shuts the door and turns to face me. I can tell he is tense and I see the stress on his face. I wish I could ask him what's wrong. I step closer to him and put my arms around his neck. "Can you believe we are going to a formal ball in Russia?" I ask him. "I know, who would've thought." He tells me. "You're not going to ditch me at the party to go talk business are you?" I ask him. He gives me a kiss on the forehead. "If I leave your side, it won't be for long, I promise." He tells me. "Good. Now let's go find me a dress."

By time we get back from the mall we have two hours before we have to leave for the party. I didn't let Derek see the dress I picked because I oddly find myself wanting to impress him. While Derek is showering I put on my makeup and fix my hair and save the dress as the finishing touch. I love the dress I picked out. It's a floor length, off the shoulder quarter sleeve black satin dress that hugs my figure with a slit down the side. It has a sweetheart neck line so it shows just the right amount of cleavage too. I feel like the black dress compliments my red hair and I am quite impressed with how good I look. Once I'm finished getting ready I put on some silver earrings and a jeweled necklace that has a camera in it, which can be activated by tapping the middle jewel. Who knows what I might come across tonight.

I hear the bathroom door open and as I turn to face Derek, I don't know who is more shocked. "You look absolutely stunning Em." Derek finally says. "Thanks." I say bashfully as I try to meet my eyes to his. "You look very handsome." I tell him. Which is an understatement. He is wearing an all black tux that molds to his physique and emphasizes his 'tall dark and handsome' appearance. His hair is a mix between styled yet messy and makes me want to run my fingers through it. "So I'd say it's safe to say, we could win sexiest couple there right?" He asks. I let out a laugh, "Quite possibly." I tell him. He comes over to me and I can smell his cologne and I have to resist the urge to take in a deep inhale. He takes my hand and prompts me to twirl, "My God, how did I get so lucky?" He tells me. I look away, but he turns my head to face his so he can look into my eyes. "Quit that." He tells me in a frustrated. "Q-q-quit what?" I stutter. "Getting embarrassed every time I compliment you. You are absolutely and irrevocably the most beautiful woman I have ever laid my eyes on." He tells me. I feel my knees get weak and Derek puts his arm around my back and his mere touch makes my whole body feel like it just caught on fire. I can feel our faces grow closer by the second as we gaze into each others eyes and just as our lips are about to touch, a sharp knock at the door interrupts us.

Derek lets go of me and goes to answer the door. I savor the time alone so I can resume my composure. None of this seems real. It's as if I'm living in some romance movie, but if he's so attracted to me, why hasn't he tried to pull a move? "Emma our ride is here." I hear Derek shout. Our ride? I make my way to the door and see a buff man I have never seen before standing in the doorway.

"Babe, this is Dimitri. He works for my new partner." I approach Dimitri, "Hi, I'm Emma." I say as I stick out my hand and he gently shakes it. "Wow, you must work out a lot." I say admirably as I feel his bicep. Derek clears his throat and I can see Dimitri shoot Derek a smug smirk. I quickly pull my hand away. "Let me just grab my purse." I say as I go to retrieve it from the bedroom. I linger at the door in hopes of overhearing any exchange of conversation.

"Let's hope for your sake, you don't slip up. I'd have fun with that one." I hear Dimitri say. "Shut the hell up. If you threaten her again, I'll kick your ass." Derek replies. Again? That explains why Derek has been so tense and over protective the last few days. "Babe is my purse in there?" I shout. After a brief pause he responds, "No, I don't see it." I wait for another minute to pass and then emerge with my purse. "Sorry, it was under the bed." I say, "It must have fell under there from earlier." I add provocatively. "We must get going." Dimitri says.

We make our way down and outside the hotel is a limo. Dimitri opens the door for me to get in. "We are going in a limo?" I ask him excitedly. "Yes ma'am." Dimitri says as he motions for me to get in. "Eww don't call me ma'am, it makes me feel old. Please, call me Emma" I tell him. "Very well Emma." He says as he puts his hand on my back and ushers me in. Despite his touch making my skin crawl, I shoot him a flirtatious smile, "Why thank you." I tell him. "My pleasure." He replies with a smile and then shuts the door.

I can tell Derek isn't happy with my overly friendly interactions with Dimitri. I scoot next to him and stare at him, but he won't look at me. I start to caress his thigh which gets his attention. "What are you doing?" He asks as he peers over at me. "Come on babe, let's have a little fun." I tell him.

"Now's not the time Em." He replies and looks back out the window. I channel every bit of courage I have and swing my legs over his and straddle his lap. He gives me a shocked expression. "Come on, they can't see us." I say, knowing damn well they can, but that's the point. "Em." He says skittishly. I start to kiss along his neck and he falls silent. I give him a soft kiss on the lips and I feel him kiss me back as his arms lock around my waist and he pulls my body closer to his. His kisses get sloppier as he makes his way down my neck and to my breasts. I can feel Derek's growing excitement and it has my body in overdrive. I feel Derek pull back and I let out a soft whimper when he stops. "What's wrong?" I ask softly. He puts his forehead to mine and lets out a sigh, "I want you so damn bad, but not right now." He says.

I can feel my face become flushed with embarrassment as I take the seat next to him. I know it's silly to be mad, especially when he's not obligated to be involved with me intimately, but this rejection stings a little more than usual. "Em, don't be mad." Derek says. I look away as I blink back the tears and remain silent. He lets out another sigh, "You think I like being left hanging? Now I'm stuck with blue balls till we get home." He says as he throws his hands up in the air. I can't help, but let out a laugh at his remark. "Oh you think that's funny?" He says as he flashes me a smile. I nod as I let out another giggle. "You won't be laughing when you have to make up for it later." He tells me with a smirk. And just like that I'm already turned on again. I purse my lips and he gives them a kiss.

Fortunately we arrive two minutes later. I don't think I would be able to control my brewing sexual tension any longer. When we pull up, it's to a large gated estate. There are a bunch of cars pulling into the round about drive way, to drop people off. When it's our turn, some other gentleman helps us out and we make our way into the house. The house is elegant inside and out. As we enter it there is already a bunch of people here. Derek puts his arm out for me to loop mine around and he escorts us further into the crowd. We gather a bunch of looks, as I'm sure we stick out like a sore thumb. A cocktail waitress comes by and we each take a glass of champagne.

Everyone around us is speaking in Russian which makes it difficult to start a conversation since we aren't supposed to know Russian. We play it safe and keep to ourselves and make commentary on the decorations and home itself. Thirty minutes later a bell rings and everyone quiets down. Everyone directs their gaze at the elaborate marble staircase at the north end of the house. Viktor Chubinsky appears at the top of stairs with a much younger female counterpart at his side. The crowd applauds as he makes his way down the staircase. Once they make it to the floor, the lights dim and the music starts.

"Well that wasn't weird at all." Derek says. I let out a laugh, "Right. That was slightly on the border of creepy." We both laugh. "See, I'm so glad we are married. We just get one another." Derek says. I can feel the butterflies fluttering in my stomach and I know it's just a part of the cover, but my pathetic little heart is swooning. "Well then I guess it's a good thing we're in this forever." I reply. We exchange a quick peck and direct our attention back on the crowd. As the tempo slows, some of the couples make their way to the dance floor for a slow dance. Derek throws back the rest of his champagne and holds out his hand. "May I have this dance?" He asks. I set down my glass and take his hand as he leads me onto the floor. He spins me once and then pulls my body to his. My hands rest on his shoulders, while his hands take their place around my waist. As the soft romantic tune plays, our bodies sway in rhythm to the melody and I can't help but feel entranced in this moment. I allow myself to inhale his scent so I can truly capture this moment and when I open my eyes I see him staring at me. He rubs his thumb along my cheek and then kisses me. I kiss him back and I let our lips linger for a few seconds before I pull away. I rest my head on his chest and we stay that way until the songs ends.

Once it's over, Derek escorts me off the floor and we take our place at one of the vacant tables. Right as the next song starts to play I feel a tap on my shoulder. I turn to see Mikhail behind me. "Mikhail, long time no see." I tell him jokingly. "My, my Emma. I must say you look stunning, Derek here is a lucky man." Mikhail says as he pats Derek on the back. "I guess we both lucked out." I say as I give Derek a smile. "Would you mind if I stole her for a dance?" Mikhail asks Derek. Derek hesitates to respond. "I promise she will be safe with me. I won't even try to steal from you." Mikhail says as he nonchalantly motions over his shoulder. I have to keep myself from looking, but I see Derek look past Mikhail and I'm sure it's a set up for Derek to go talk with Viktor.

"Oh I suppose I can spare her for a little while, as long as Emma doesn't mind." Derek says. Mikhail looks at me, "Not at all." I say cheerily. Mikhail bows and then puts his hand out.

Mikhail leads me out to the dance floor and while doing so I turn on the camera, just incase I can get any valuable intel. Luckily the tune isn't as slow but it's still a romantic melody for us to dance to. Mikhail respectfully opts for holding my one hand while his other hand rests on my hip. I can tell Mikhail isn't exactly the slow dance type, as all of his steps are hurried and too soon. When we turn, I can now see Dimitri talking with Derek and I wish I could hear what they are saying. I see Dimitri point upstairs and I can only assume he's telling Derek to meet upstairs.

"So Viktor lives in this huge house?" I ask Mikhail. "Yep." "It's so beautiful. I hope one day me and Derek can have a house like this." I tell him. He laughs, "I'm sure you will. Derek doing business with Viktor might make that happen a lot sooner than you think." "Really?" I say giving him a big grin. "Really. Partnering with Viktor was a smart business move for your husband." "Apparently. Was that him, the one that came down the stairs?" "Yes, that would be him." "Please tell me that's not his wife though, she looks young and he's well, no offense, but old and icky." Mikhail lets out a big laugh, "Looks go away, but money is constant. It's just that some women prefer the value of the later." Mikhail tells me. "I beg to differ Mikhail. If you spend the money, then it'll be gone. So you might as well enjoy the view while the money lasts." "You are one interesting woman." Mikhail says as he lets out another chuckle and shakes his head. "I guess I just want my cake, and I want to eat it too." I shrug. "As do most women. You were fortunate to get the best of both worlds, but if you ever want more, you always have more options." Mikhail tells me. "What do you mean?" I ask him inquisitively. "Forgive me for my forwardness Emma. A guy can only dream to have the pleasure of the companionship of a woman like you. I was simply stating if Derek does not fulfill all of your desires, I'm sure there is a man out there who can do so." Mikhail tells me. I am indeed baffled by his bluntness. "I appreciate you looking out for my wellbeing Mikhail, but I do love my husband. Very much so and I would be heartbroken if I were to ever lose him." I tell Mikhail. "Then for your sake, I urge you to keep your husband in Viktor's good graces." Mikhail whispers to me. "Wait, what is that supposed to mean?" I say trying to play dumb. He twirls me and gives me a big smile, "I don't know what you are talking about, you are quite an excellent dancer Emma." Mikhail tells me. At that time the song ends and Mikhail leads me back off the dance floor.

"Would you like a drink?" Mikhail asks me. "No I would like you to elaborate on what you just told me." I tell him. If I can get him to explain the type of business Viktor is involved in then this could be the solidifying evidence we need to take down Viktor and his men. "Heed my warning Emma, Viktor is not a man Derek wants to cross. The type of business Viktor is involved in is dangerous and not always legal. It puts Derek and you at risk." "Why are you telling me this? Does Derek know?" I say frantically. Mikhail waves over a cocktail waitress. "Calm your expressions or you will draw attention. You remind me a lot of my late wife and I'd hate to see anything happen to you too." He says. "So that's how you two met, very interesting." Mikhail says as he grabs us each a drink. I am shocked at Mikhail's words, as it alludes to the assumption that Viktor killed Mikhail's wife and I actually feel kind of sorry for him. I take the drink and give a slight bow, "Thank you for the lovely dance Mikhail." I tell him. "The pleasure is mine." Mikhail says as he delivers a parting kiss to my free hand.

As Mikhail disappears, I am left alone. It's not long before I am approached by a man I have never seen before. The man asks if I'd like to dance in Russian, but I reply, "I'm sorry, I don't speak Russian." The man gives a scoff of disgust and walks off. "Rude." I murmur to myself. "He was asking if you'd like to dance." Dimitri says, startling me. "Oh my gosh you scared me." I say. "Sorry." Dimitri says gruffly. "Where is Derek? I went to dance with Mikhail and now he's gone." I say. "He went to go talk over some matters with the boss." Dimitri replies. "Actually they are partners." I say matter of factly. Dimitri actually cracks a smile and gives a half laugh, "We all work for the boss. Including you, you just don't know it yet." "Excuse me? I do not work for anybody." I tell him blatantly. "That'll change." He says followed by a smirk. I start to look around to make my discomfort known. "He'll be back when the boss lets him go." Dimitri says. I let out a large sigh, "He promised me he wouldn't leave me to go talk business tonight." "Then I guess I'll just have to keep you company in the meantime."

Dimitri says. I roll my eyes, "I doubt you'd be of any good company." I tell him. "There's only one way to find out." He says as he takes a step closer to me, making me feel uncomfortable. It's not like I can just outright kick his ass without blowing our cover, so I have no choice but to keep playing along. "And what exactly do you have in mind?" I ask as I trace his bicep with my finger. He lets out a cocky huff, "Well for starters, I can pick up where you left off in the limo." I let out an astonished gasp and turn around to pretend to hide my embarrassment. "Nothing to be ashamed of. It's apparent your needs aren't being met and I can help you with that." He says as he caresses my arm. I turn around slowly to face him. "I-I-I'm a married woman." I stammer. "It can be our little secret." He whispers.

I give him a mischievous grin as I try to think of a response, but I suddenly feel a firm hand on my back. I can tell it's Derek's and I turn to show my relief when I notice he has a cut to his bottom lip. "Derek, you're lip." I say with concern. "It's fine, I just took a wrong turn." My blood begins to boil, because I know that's not the case. I should have been there to have his back. "Are you sure?" I say as I reach up to touch it. He grabs my hand and shoves it back down. "I said it's fine Emma. You need to learn your place." He tells me harshly. I try to hide the shock and hurt that his words deliver, but I can't hold it back. As the tears well in my eyes, I smack him and storm off.

I know I shouldn't take his words to heart but, as of right now I don't know what's real or not. This is why I prefer working alone. Partners get in the way and in this case, get in my head. My lines of reality are so blurred that it's hard for me to decipher Derek's true feelings for me. Great, I can see it now, I'm going to be *that spy*, that they all make fun of. I worked too hard for this. I make a beeline to the bathroom and lock myself in.

After about fifteen minutes I pull myself together and emerge from the bathroom. While doing so I bump into the girl that was with Viktor. "Sorry." I say as I wipe my eyes in attempt to fix my smudged makeup. "Oh dear, are you okay?" She asks in a heavy Russian accent. "I'm fine. I just got in a fight with my husband." I sob, hoping she'll pay pity to me. "Come. Let's fix your make up." She says while offering me a soft smile. I give her a pitiful nod and I follow her as she leads me up a hidden set of stairs. She leads me into a massive bedroom and I stop to gawk. "Wait, do you live here?" I ask stupidly. She laughs, "Yes I do. This is my room." She says. "It's magnificent." I say in awe. "Thank you. Now follow me." She ushers me into a large bathroom with a fully equipped vanity and motions for me to take a seat. I sit down as she starts pulling out a bunch of makeup. "You are too pretty to be crying over stupid man." She says as she starts to powder my face. I give a sniffle, "I just didn't think he was like that. We just got married three weeks ago." I say as I hold up my ring for her to see. "That is what men do. They trick you to make you believe what they want and then show their true colors once you're trapped." She says. I look in the mirror and can see her try to hide her saddened expression. This might be my chance to get some dirt on Viktor. "So you're married to an asshole too?" I say, prompting her to laugh. "Yes, but I guarantee yours is not as bad as mine." She says. "Try me." I say. I can tell she is scared to reply as she hesitates to look around. "It's okay, you don't have to tell me, it's your business not mine." I tell her. She gives me warm smile and starts to fix my eyeliner. "Beautiful!" She exclaims once she's finished. I look in the mirror and turn to give her a big smile, "Thank you so much." I tell her softly and give her a hug. "I'm so glad I met you, my name is Emma." I tell her. "Emma, as in Derek Matthews wife?" "Yes..." I say leerily. "Sorry, I had just overheard Viktor and his men mention your names. Just glad I can put a face with the name." She says. "Oh. Yeah Derek and Viktor are business partners now." I tell her. She lowers her voice, "Whatever you do, do not let Viktor or his men get you alone." She tells me and I can see the panic on her face. I give her a nod. "Maybe now that they are partners, we can hang out while they handle business." I suggest. She gives me a sorrow filled look, "As much as I'd like that, you'd do best to steer clear of me and anything to do with Viktor or he will enroll you too." "Enroll me in what?" I ask her. "RDSR." She says almost silently. This is exactly what I needed. Now we just need the visual proof before Derek can make an arrest. "Now come. We have been gone long enough, they will notice we are both missing soon. She quickly leads us out the room and stops at the end of the stairs. "Go find your husband and stay close to him." She tells me and then turns to go back up the stairs. "Wait." I hiss. She glances over her shoulder. "What is your name?" I ask her. "Nadia." She whispers. "Thank you Nadia." I tell her, she nods and then hurries up the stairs.

I hide my excitement as I make my way through the crowd. I just got solid supporting evidence that Viktor is involved with the Russian drug smuggling ring. Now if Derek can just get the visual proof then we can go forward with the bust. I finally spot Derek across the way and I can already see the frantic look on his face.

I approach him with caution as I know he's probably pissed at me for running off. I tap his shoulder and he quickly spins around to face me. We both stare at each other for a moment before he embraces me. "Where have you been? I have been worried sick about you." He tells me. "I went to the bathroom so I could cry in peace." I tell him as I push him away to show that I'm still mad at him. We stare at one other once again and the guilt starts to settle in. Here I go smacking him after he just got his lip busted when all he was trying to do was keep his cover. "I'm sorry." We both blurt out at the same time. "No, I'm sorry. I shouldn't have talked to you that way." Derek says and then clears his throat before continuing, "But, I need you to understand that as the man of the house, what I say goes. A lot of my clients and investors are men of prestige and power and I need to have the same mentality as them if I want to be like them." "I understand. I'm sorry for slapping you." I tell him. "Good, now let's say we get out of here and go make some fun of our own." He says with a wink. I give him a teasing grin followed by a kiss that makes him wince. I pretend as if I didn't see it and let Derek guide me through the crowd.

Just as we are about to reach the door, I hear Derek's name called. "Leaving so soon Derek?" I hear a man say. We both turn around to see Viktor Chubinsky with Dimitri at his side. He is short and plump with a pepper gray goatee and who knows many gold chains he has around his stubby neck. "Ah Viktor. Yes, unfortunately I had already made prior engagements with the wife." Derek tells him. I try not to notice Viktor's disgusting eyes looking me up and down. "That's right, a promise is a promise." I say as I look up at Derek and grab ahold of his hand. Dimitri scoffs, and speaks aloud in Russian. "She's a filthy whore. She's been practically begging him to have sex with her." I instantly feel Derek squeeze my hand so tight that my fingers become numb and I take it as sign that Derek can speak Russian. As sweet as it is to see Derek get upset and protective over me, I'd love to give Dimitri a good ass whooping myself. It's times like these that make keeping your composure and cover under wraps real difficult. Viktor throws his hand up, "Dimitri, manners. Our guests don't understand Russian." He says before directing his gaze back on me and extends his hand out to me. I give a polite smile and offer him my hand. Viktor then pulls me away from Derek and closer to him. "You must be Mrs. Matthews." Viktor says. "The one and only." I tell him followed with a bright smile. "I've heard so much about you, but they failed to mention exactly just how beautiful you are." I muster a blush in response to his compliment. "Why thank you Mr. Chubinsky." I tell him. He lets out deep chuckle. "Please, call me Viktor. After all, I have a feeling we are going to get quite acquainted now that your husband and I are business partners." He says as he gives me a spine chilling smile. "My apologies Viktor. I hope you forgive us for leaving so early, this is truly a lovely party." I tell him. "No worries, I'm pleased to hear you enjoyed your time." He says. After he kisses my hand, he releases me from his hold and I take my spot back at Derek's side. "Dimitri, see to it that this lovely couple make it back safely." Dimitri gives him a nod and then escorts us out of the house.

The car ride home is uneventful and silent. When we make it back to the hotel we try to make a quick escape, but Dimitri cuts us off. "Not so fast." He tells us. "The boss wanted me to give you this." Dimitri says as he hands Derek what appears to be a burner phone. "You should see to it that you don't miss any of his calls." He adds. Derek takes the phone and just gives him a nod before pushing his way past Dimitri. As I follow Derek, Dimitri grabs me by the arm and pulls me close and whispers to me, "Don't forget about my offer." He then lets me go and gives my ass a small pat. I shoot him a daggering look and he just gives me a perverted smile. Luckily Derek doesn't see, as he's already to the door.

Chapter 13: Liam

I am relieved when we finally make it up to the room. It killed me having to treat Emma the way I did. While Mikhail took Emma to dance, Dimitri took me to meet with Chubinsky. They gave me a not so friendly initiation to the crew. Afterwards they told me that I need to assert my dominance over Emma so that way she wouldn't go meddling into our business affairs. I can't tell if I truly hurt her feelings or not, but the slap sure felt believable.

Emma looks so somber as she makes her way into the bedroom. I'm not sure if I should follow her or give her some space. In hopes of getting things back to normal, I follow her into the room. When I enter the room she stops and stares at me for moment before continuing to take off her jewelry. I approach her from behind and she looks at me in the mirror.

"I'm sorry for tonight." I tell her. "It's fine." She replies. I let out a deep sigh, unsure of what else to say. "Despite the shitty ending, I truly enjoyed everything up till the end of our dance." I tell her. I can see a small smile come across her face for a brief moment and that at least lets me know she agrees. There's nothing else for me to say, so I turn to go get changed. "Derek." Emma says softly. I turn back face her, "Yes?" She looks back at me, "Would you unzip me?" She asks. "Of course." I reply as I step behind her once more. I slowly unzip her dress and I can't help but admire my view as more and more of her body is revealed. I see the back of her black lace bra and the top of her matching panties and it has my mind racing. It instantly reminds me of our brief rendezvous in the limo. What I'd give to pick up where we left off. "Thank you." She says as she holds up her dress and makes her way to the bathroom.

I take this time as an opportunity to go to the gym. I have so some serious frustration and tension I need to release and working up a good sweat helps with that. I do about forty-five minutes of cardio and thirty minutes on the punching bag. I'd be lying if I said I didn't imagine Dimitri as the bag. I can let his initiation ass kicking slide, but talking about Emma that way, I can't let slide. That asshole may have gotten away with it for now, but just wait until I get the chance to take him down.

By time I get back, Emma is now laying in bed reading. I do my best not to disturb her as I slip into the bathroom to shower. The hot water feels good as it rolls down my body and I welcome the extra sweat as I take advantage of my makeshift sauna. When I get out I realize I forgot to grab clean clothes so I wrap the towel around my waist and emerge from the bathroom. I see Emma glance over at me and then quickly look away. I gather my clothes and head back to the bathroom.

Once, I finish I go lay down next to Emma. I'm not usually the clingy type, but I just want to be close to Emma. Even more so now that we are in some sort of silent fight. I lay on my stomach and drape one arm over her and close my eyes. About a minute passes before I hear Emma speak. "I think we should take things to the next level." She says. I raise up quickly and turn to face her. "What?" I say in confusion. She cocks her head while keeping her eyes locked on mine. "You heard me, I want to take things to the next level tonight." She tells me while blinking excessively and then it hits me. That was our set code phrase to indicate that we have supporting evidence and need to focus on getting the physical proof. "Are you sure?" I ask her. "I'm positive." She tells me. "Well, then come over here." I say as I pat the empty space next to me. She puts her book down and scoots over to occupy the vacant space next to me and lays down. I lay down next to her and wrap my arms around her to pull her close. I rest my cheek on the top of her head and as we lay there I pray for this moment to never end.

We must have fallen asleep just like that because the next thing I know I'm waking up to tiny rays of sun shining through the curtain. I look down and Emma is still in my arms. It's apparent my sexual urges are raging because all I can think about is rolling on top of her and giving her a nice morning wake up call. As if the morning wood I fetched wasn't enough. I let out a silent groan and try to slide out from under her, but she puts her arm over me and snuggles closer. How can I leave this? I think to myself, so I stay put and cuddle her back. I nuzzle my face in her neck and I can tell my stubble tickles her as she lets out a soft giggle. How is it that she's so close yet so far away? I find myself wishing to wake up next her like this every morning and then the question dawns on me. Is this what love feels like? I've never been the mushy-gushy type and honestly never saw myself as the husband type. I mean hell I could care less if Anna never came around again, but with Emma, there could be a room full of women and it would still feel empty without her in it. They say you never know a person is the one until you just feel it one day, but how do I know Emma's the one?

My thoughts are interrupted when I feel Emma stretch and I feel her hand glide up my chest and comes to halt when it reaches my cheek. Emma jolts up and retracts her hand and she looks down at me. "Good morning beautiful." I tell her with a sleepy smile. "Good morning. Sorry for, erm, crowding your space." She says. I prop myself up on one elbow and look right at her. "You could take every bit of oxygen from me and I still wouldn't mind." I say. She gives a bashful smirk with a stern side eye. "Then that would be your demise." She tells me. "Death for you would be an honor." I reply. Her cheeks turn rosy as she tries to fight the smile.

She goes to get up, but I grab her arm and pull her back into bed. "Where do you think you're going?" I ask her. "To get ready for the day." She giggles. "I didn't say you could do that, now did I?" I tell her. "Well no, but you didn't tell me not to either." She says. "How about we just stay in bed today, it's not like we have anything else to do." I tell her. Famous last words, I think to myself when I hear an unfamiliar ring come from the nightstand. We both look over and see the burner phone Dimitri gave me, ringing. I quickly roll over and answer the phone.

"This is Matthews." I say. Emma scoots up against me so she can listen. "Viktor wants you over for lunch. He's got some things to go over. Be sure to bring your wife." Dimitri says. "What time?" I ask. "Noon and don't be late." He says and then I hear a click. I press the end button a couple times to make sure the call ended. "Well so much for staying in bed all day." I tell Emma. I turn and give her a peck on the lips and then hop out of bed so it seems habitual.

"Get ready we are meeting with my partner for lunch at noon." I tell her. "Should I dress up or just be casual?" She asks. "I don't know Emma, you're not a child, I shouldn't have to tell how to dress." I watch her open her mouth to respond, but then she stops. She just gets up and goes to pull out some clothes. It kills me to be rude to her, especially when I know it's not in her nature to be submissive. It's just easier for me to get in the role before we even get there so it seems more natural.

Chapter 14: Stella

Usually I'd be excited to be having direct interaction with the mission's proclaimed *bad guy*. However, Derek is a total dick when he's around them. Logically, I know it's part of the mission, but my stupid feelings seem to have been interfering with my voice of reason here lately. At least I'm prepared this time, I know that's not how he really feels, he's just doing his job. At least that's what I want to believe.

When we pull up to Viktor's place, another one of his henchman greet us in the driveway. Without saying a word he leads us inside and now that it's empty it seems so much bigger and all the more eery. The guy frisks Derek and goes to frisk me. "Hey man, don't touch my wife." Derek tells him sternly. "I don't answer to you." The man says provokingly and Derek just clenches his teeth. "Men, men, no need for the hostility." Viktor says as he appears at the top of the stairs. "Nicholai, what have I told you about putting your hands on things that aren't yours." Viktor says. "Sorry boss." The man says as he hangs his head and steps away from us. "So how is my favorite couple today?" Viktor says as he makes his way down the stairs. "We are great, thank you for inviting us over." I reply excitedly. "Excellent! Unfortunately, lunch isn't quite ready yet, so I was hoping to borrow your husband for a few words about the business launch. I hope you don't mind." Viktor tells me. I look at Derek, "I suppose I can spare him for a few minutes." I say followed by a small laugh. Viktor offers a laugh in return, "Very well. Derek if you'll follow me. Emma please make yourself comfortable. Nicholai fetch this beautiful lady whatever she desires." "You got it boss." He says with a nod. I watch Derek follow Viktor upstairs and I can't help but worry for him. I try to see exactly where they go but I can't see entirely without looking suspicious.

"Would you like something to drink?" Nicholai asks me. "Um, sure. Just a glass of water will be fine." I tell him. He walks off and disappears through a door at the far end of the room. I take a seat in a large velvet lined chair and look around to see if I notice anything out of the ordinary. I hear the door squeak and see Nicholai approaching me with a glass of water. "Thank you." I tell him as I take the glass from him. He just gives me a nod and then takes a couple steps back. It's apparent he is tasked with watching me so might as well see what I can get out of him. I take a sip of the water and set it on the end table. "So do you live here too?" I ask him in attempt to make conversation. He scoffs, "No this is the boss's house." "Oh, that's surprising, he seems like the type who would want his butlers to live with him." I say and I can tell I struck a nerve. "I'm not a butler you dumb woman." I let my mouth fall open to show my fake offense. "Well whatever you are, you should be fired for talking to his guests like that." He gives a hysterical laugh, "That's not the way it works here." He tells me. I cross my arms and turn away from him. "Why don't you go fetch Dimitri. He's more tolerable than you at this point." I tell him. Nicholai laughs, "That's because Dimitri is a sucker to any pretty bimbo that walks by, like you." I shoot him a glare and imagine giving him a roundhouse kick to the temple. "I'm not scared of you." I tell him. He swiftly yanks my hair back and pins my head to the back of the chair. "You should be." He whispers in my ear and I can smell the stench of cigarettes and vodka on his breath. For the sake of protecting our cover, I refrain from kicking his ass. Instead I grab the cup of water off the table and throw it on him. He lets go and I quickly stand up to face him. Great, I can tell I only pissed him off even more. "You bitch." He sputters as he wipes the water from his face. "Wait until I tell Viktor about this." I shout. Nicholai gives a menacing laugh, "He doesn't care about you, you dumb whore." "Really? What if I told him I heard you take a suspicious call about taking some money off the top on the next deal?" I threaten. He gives me a snarl, "You wouldn't dare." He says. I bat my eyes, "Why would I lie? I'm just a dumb whore." I reply mockingly. "What do you want?" He asks seethingly. "I want you to leave me the hell alone." I tell him. He lets out a low growl, "You're lucky I need to go change. Sit and don't move a muscle." He orders me. "Not till your out of my personal space." I say with a smug look. He lets out a large huff, to signal his loss and storms off. I sit and stay there until I hear the door squeak. I look around to scan my surroundings and note my exit routes before I make my way quickly up the stairs. I make sure to be light on my feet to avoid any creaks on the wooden floor. I go in the direction I saw Viktor and Derek go. I'm hoping to overhear some of their conversation and record it so it can be used as evidence. We figured Derek would be patted down so he couldn't wear a wire, but the recorders for most of the female agents are quite discrete. As I get closer to the south end of the hall I pick up on Derek and Viktor's voice. I click the hair pin holding my hair back and it starts the recorder. As I get closer I can finally make out what they are saying.

"So all I have to do is turn a blind eye to the accounts you'll be operating over and you'll let me keep sixty percent of the cuts on all the transactions?" Derek says. "Correct." Viktor says. "What's the catch?" Derek replies. "What do you mean?" Viktor asks. "It sounds too good to be true, so what's the fine print?" Derek asks. "There's no catch. Your business will make my transactions appear legal to the government's eye, which provides the perfect cover for my business affairs on the side." Viktor states. "Will the money disclosed from your side affairs be included in my sixty percent?" Derek asks. Viktor is silent for a couple seconds, "Eventually, but you'll need to earn my trust first." "Fine. But how do I know you won't screw me over?" Derek asks. Viktor laughs, "Because I don't need your money, I invested because I want to capitalize on the profits." "Exactly, you just said my business is allowing you to make your profits more easily, so how do I know you won't try to take over my assets?" Derek tells him. "Simple, you don't interfere with my assets, I won't interfere with yours." Viktor replies. "Fair enough." Derek states. "Now that we got that settled, how would you feel about Emma working with my wife and some other women to help increase our sales and profit?" "What are you suggesting?" Derek asks. "Sometimes I allow Nadia to go off with some of my lonelier clients for periods of time as an added benefit to, let's just say, make the clients happier and in turn we can charge them more. Emma would be the perfect fresh meat to entice new clientele." "Are you asking me to pimp my wife out Viktor?" "I'm not saying right away, but it's something to think about. Since I brought on Nadia, profits have increased by twenty percent." "I don't know Viktor. I mean how are you even okay with sharing your woman with other men." Viktor lets out another laugh, "You don't drive the same cars that you loan out my friend. And from what I hear, you have no problem turning down Emma's advances anyway, so it's apparent she's not fulfilling your urges like she should be. Maybe it's time you let her be of use somehow." Derek is silent. "Just throwing it out there. I know this is your honeymoon so I won't expect an answer anytime soon." Viktor adds. "I just don't think she'll be of much use honestly. I mean yeah she's got sex appeal, but once you get her in the sac it's like she has no idea what she's doing. It's not pleasurable at all. Hell she can't even cook. It's good thing you invited us over otherwise I'd have to pretend to enjoy another one her meals." Derek says and they both erupt with laughter. I instantly get a lump in my throat as my eyes start to tear up. Of course, he can't speak from experience, but to assume I'm not good in bed because I don't have much experience is offensive. Then to add the cherry on top he insulted my cooking. Yeah I'm not the greatest cook, but I've been trying and to hear him say that he has to pretend to like it, hurts. It's apparent I don't have the qualities he wants in a woman, I can't believe I let my stupid emotions convince me otherwise. What a douche. I make my silent retreat before I hear anything else that will kill my confidence. I start to cry as I make my way down the main staircase.

"Where where you? I told you not to move." I hear Nicholai say angrily when he spots me. I wipe my tears as I shove past him. "Where the hell do you think you're going?" He asks. "I'm leaving!" I shout. He lets out a cackle, "Awe, did princess hear something she didn't like." He shouts back. I walk straight out the door and then realize I don't have the key. Screw it, I'll just walk.

As I'm approaching the iron gate, it starts to open and a blacked out car pulls up and stops in front of me. The passenger side window rolls and Dimitri gives me a disturbing smile. "Well look who it is." He says. "Yeah and?" I reply, making it apparent I am not in the mood for his antics right now. "Oh someone's feisty today." "Yeah and now I'm leaving." I tell him as I continue to walk around the car. I hear the car door open, but before I can turn around Dimitri puts me in a hold from behind and jams a needle in my neck. Next thing I know, I feel my body go limp as the world around me fades to black.

When I come through, I have a pounding headache and it takes a minute for my eyes to adjust to the dark room. I feel my heart racing as I start to itch my neck where Dimitri sedated me. I get up off the bed and thoroughly look over my body. I let out a sigh of relief at the realization they didn't take advantage of me, but notice a track mark to my right arm. I can only imagine what they've given me. I start to wonder how long I've been out, there's no windows in this room. I approach the door and put my ear up to it to see if I can hear anyone on the outside. There's no door knob so it must be the exit. I go to the only other door in the room and turn the knob. It just leads to a small half bathroom and I take the opportunity to take a quick pee. When I'm done I go back into the main room and look around. The room is small and basic. It has a bed and a night stand that holds an empty cup. This must be the rooms Viktor keeps the women he sells off. I smirk at the thought that he now has another charge against him. We had no idea he was involved in human trafficking as well, but it doesn't surprise me either.

There's nothing else to do so I just plop down on the bed and think about the situation at hand. It's hard to say if our covers are blown, but I feel like they would've just put a bullet in me if that was the case. Which means, they plan to get me hooked on whatever it is they are selling and use it as leverage to force me to do what they want. And how long do they think they can keep me here without Derek noticing?

I get up and go back to the door. "Helloooo." I say. There's no response. I bang on the door repeatedly, still nothing. Interesting, they don't even have anyone here to guard me. Either that or they are ordered to ignore me. I glance at my watch and debate activating the distress signal that will register to Derek's watch and give him my location. It's not like I'm in immediate danger at the moment though. Besides, he hasn't emitted his distress signal so it's safe to say our covers are still intact. The watches also have a button to alarm when a covers been blown. This signals to the base that an extraction is needed and at that point it's every agent for themself and they are ordered to get to the extraction point as soon as possible.

After two hours, I hear a soft thud that makes my ears perk. I quickly get up and go over to the door. I hear the faint shuffling of feet and I can see a shadow stop in front of my door. I hear a piece of metal clink and a hissing sound, followed by a cloud of gas that starts to appear from under the door. I run to the far side of the room and take a pillowcase and wrap it around my face. The room starts to fill with gas and I can't escape it any longer. I start to get dizzy and lightheaded and feel myself drop to the floor. I'm barely conscious, but through hazy vision I see the door open and a figure enter the room. The figure comes over to me and nudges me with their foot. They grab my arm and I wince as I feel a needle shoved in my arm. The figure crouches down next to me and whispers, "Tell Derek he knows what he needs to do and this will stop." I recognize the voice, "Mikhail" I barely manage to say as I reach out for him. He stands up and backs away, "Bring him in." Mikhail shouts.

The door opens once more and I see another dark figure enter the room and run over to me. "Emma" I hear Derek say as he kneels down next to me. "What did you do?" Derek shouts angrily. Mikhail ignores his question "We'll give you two some time." Mikhail says and leaves the room.

"Emma can you hear me?" Derek asks. I manage to nod. He scoops me up and carries me over to the bed. He lays me gently on the bed and I see him start to pace the room. "Derek" I say weakly. He runs over to me, "Hey, hey, what is it? What can I do?" He says frantically. "Water" I say as I manage to point to the bathroom. He grabs the glass and hurries to the bathroom. When he returns he raises me up and helps me take a sip. "Try to rest." He tells me as he pulls the covers over me. That's the last thing I remember before I pass out.

When I wake up, I sit up and see Derek sitting at the end of the bed. "Derek." I say. He turns around and I see a look of relief fall across his face. He comes over to me and I can see his eyes are red and puffy as if he had been crying. "How are you feeling?" He asks "My head is killing me." I reply. He brushes my hair out of the way and traces my cheek with his thumb. "I was so worried about you." He tells me and I can tell his words are genuine. I give him a hug, "I'll be okay, but you know what you need to do." I tell him. He pulls away, "You don't know what they are asking me to do Em." He says. "Then tell me so we can figure it out together." I tell him. "Viktor says I can be a part of one of his direct deals tomorrow night." He says. I give him a confused look, this is exactly what we need in order for Derek to call in for the arrest. "Babe isn't that a good thing?" I tell him. He takes a hard swallow, "But, in order for me to go, I have to let them take you away. You'll be drugged, stripped down and sold to one of Viktor's clients tomorrow morning." Now I take a hard swallow. That means I'd be long gone with no way for my location to be traced before Derek would even be able to make the bust. Which means, I'd have to sacrifice myself in order for Derek to take down Viktor Chubinsky once and for all. Either that or abort the mission just so we can both make it back safely. We silently stare at one another for a long time, as we both understand the gravity of the situation. "Maybe it's time we think about our other options." Derek finally says he looks at his watch and I know that he's indicating for us to signal an extraction. I get up and walk over to the opposite side of the room as I ponder our only two options.

I have no family with no ties to anyone. The only person who cares about me is Kat, but she knows more than anybody how important my job is to me. I've busted my ass to rise up from nothing and make a name for myself. I'm not going to let some chump scare me into backing out of a mission, even if it's the last thing I do. Taking Chubinsky down will be the biggest bust since the fifties and it'll eliminate the threat to our national security. I would gladly sacrifice myself for the safety of my country.

I turn around to face him. "No. You've worked too hard to back down now." I tell him, "think of our future." I add. He walks over to me and cups my head in his hands, "It's not worth it. I want you all to myself." He tells me. We lock eyes and I can see the distress on his face and for a split second I contemplate changing my mind. I shake my head. I can't let him convince me otherwise. I break free from his hold, "I won't let you throw it all away for me." I tell him sternly. He opens his mouth to respond, but I hold up my hand. "End of discussion. Don't make me tell Viktor myself." I tell him. He hangs his head in defeat and I take my place on the bed. I draw my knees up to my chest and tuck my head in my lap as I try to process what this means for me. After a few minutes pass I feel Derek sit down next to me.

Despite the amount of stress I am under, his presence is soothing. I start to imagine what life would be like if our outcome was different and we ended up together. I imagine us being lazy and laying wrapped up in each other's arms on a Sunday morning so we wouldn't have to move until one of us had to pee. I imagine his kisses and how the amount of spark I feel with one kiss could probably bring me back to life. I wish I could tell him how I feel and ask him if he felt the same way. That would be my only regret out of this whole thing.

I raise my head and look over at him and he gives me a sullen look. I cup his cheek with my hand and give him a soft smile, "Lets not waste what little time we have being gloomy." I tell him. He takes a deep breathe and lets it out slowly. "You're right." He tells me with a forced half smile. "Could you hold me?" I ask. He gives me his heart stopping smile and opens his arms and I let him pull me close. He kisses me on the forehead and squeezes me tight. We lay there for a moment before Derek breaks the silence.

"Do you regret it?" He asks. I look up at him, "Regret what?" "Marrying me. Coming to Russia. I don't know, just our time together in general I guess." I can't tell if he's fishing for my true feelings our trying to tame the guilt he's probably feeling. Regardless this is my chance to express how I feel. "Even if I knew the outcome all along, I would still do it, because I at least got to have you in my life." I tell him as I hug him a little tighter. "Emma." "Yes Derek." "I need to see those beautiful blue eyes of yours." I look up once more and meet the intense twinkle of his hazel eyes.

"Even if all we have is tonight, then I'm going to love you till the morning light." Derek whispers. My heart flutters at his proclamation and then I feel his lips collide with mine. This is the moment I have secretly hoped for since the first time we kissed and now that I have nothing else to lose, there is no holding back.

I kiss him back passionately and then as the lust builds up our kiss is quickly exchanged for hasty sloppy kisses. He rolls me onto my back and as he hovers over me I eagerly slip his shirt off. I take a moment to admire my view while I run my hands down his sculpted chest. He kisses each side of my neck as he works his way down. I feel his hand slide under me and undo my bra which prompts me to take off my shirt. Once he has taken in his new territory he continues his trail of kisses as he fondles my breasts. I let out a soft groan to indicate my approval. I let my hands work their way down and I'm greeted by a large bulge and now I find myself frustratingly tugging on his pants. He grabs my hands and pins them above my head. He leans down and kisses my neck softly, "Are you sure?" He whispers and his warm breathy words trigger goosebumps to form across my entire body. "I've never been more sure." I tell him encouragingly. He releases my hands and they immediately return to undo his pants. Before I manage to slide down his boxers he sits back and unbuttons my pants. I raise my hips so he can pull them off, leaving us both in nothing but our underwear. I give him a pouty face and pull him back on top of me. He gives me another long kiss as he slips my panties off. Not wanting to waste any more time, I pull down his boxers and to my pleasure, reveal how well endowed he is. I catch myself holding my breath until he enters me and when he does so we both let out a groan. He slowly takes over my body and once I've taken all of him his thrusts start to get faster. I cry out in pleasure which only makes him go harder. My nails sink into his back in hopes of keeping myself from orgasming. He uses his free hand to play with my breasts while he continues to thrust in and out of me and my body is on the brink of ecstasy. I don't remember sex ever feeling this good. "I can't hold off any longer." I cry out. It's as if that was his cue, because he doesn't hold back anymore and it's as if his thrusts have shifted into over drive. My body begins to tremble and I let out a large moan as I orgasm and when I do so Derek lets out a groan and his eyes roll back.

He collapses next to me as we both pant for air. He looks over at me and I give him a big smile. He flashes me his smile that I adore so much. We turn to face each other and he presses his sweaty forehead to mine. "You are absolutely amazing." He tells me. I give him a kiss, "You're telling me we could've been doing that this whole time?" I tell him playful. He lets out a small laugh as he twirls my hair around his finger. "I don't think it'll ever be the same now." He tells me. We lay entwined together for about ten minutes before we both get up to get dressed. Once we are re-dressed, we lay on the bed once more as Derek holds me until we fall asleep.

It's not till I feel myself being ripped away from Derek's grasp that I wake up. I look up and see Dimitri and Nicholai pulling me off the bed. "Let her go." Derek shouts. "Put me down." I say as I try to wiggle free from their hold. "You made your decision." Dimitri tells Derek. Nicholai grabs my legs and uses a rope to tie them together while Dimitri bounds my hands behind my back. Derek delivers a punch to Nicholai's jaw. Nicholai gives a sadistic laugh as he wipes the blood from his lip, "Keep it up and will tell the boss you refused his offer." Derek clenches his jaw as he knows he has no choice, but to let them take me. "It'll be okay." I tell Derek reassuringly. Nicholai scoffs, "Well aren't you just precious." He says as he grabs me by the neck and takes in one long inhale. Derek takes a step toward Nicholai, but he whips around. "Uh, uh, uh. I wouldn't do that if I were you." Nicholai says as he wags his finger at Derek. Derek comes to a halt and I can sense is feeling of helplessness. Dimitri throws me over his shoulder and carries me away. Just as Derek disappears from my sight I see him shed a single tear.

When we exit the building I notice we are surrounded by trees and appear to be in the middle of nowhere. "Where are you taking me?" I ask. "Shut it." Nicholai chirps. "This isn't necessary, I can walk." I say. Nicholai delivers a hard smack to my face. "You don't call the shots here." He tells me. I spit in his face, "And neither do you." I say snidely. I see Nicholai cock back his fist and I prepare myself for the impact of his punch. Dimitri quickly turns and takes the blunt of the punch. "Do you want to answer to the boss as to why you defied his instructions?" He says firmly. Nicholai mutters under his breath as he walks past us. "Thank you." I whisper to Dimitri. "Keep quiet if you know what's good for you." He tells me. After a few minutes we approach a car and

Dimitri sets me down and opens the trunk. "Get in." He says. "You're joking." I reply. "Get in or I'll put you in there myself." Dimitri says. I reluctantly fall back into the trunk and Nicholai flashes me a devilish grin as he shuts the trunk on me.

After what feels like an hour, the car comes to a complete stop and I hear two doors open and shut. The trunk pops open and Dimitri and Nicholai are standing over me. "Let me do it." Nicholai says as he holds out his hand. Dimitri rolls his eyes as he hands Nicholai a syringe. I try to scoot further back in the trunk, but it's not use, he jams the needle into my neck and within three seconds everything fades to black.

I feel groggy as I start to regain consciousness. I look down and see myself tied to a chair and as my vision becomes less blurry I see that I'm in a warehouse of some sort. The windows don't offer much clue to my surrounding area, but I can see that it's dark. I wonder if Derek has made the arrest yet.

"She's awake." I hear an unfamiliar voice say. I let out a groan as I muster up the strength to speak. "Where am I?" I ask. A man, who I assume to be another one of Viktor's henchmen, comes around to face me and I can see that he has a gun draped across his chest. "Don't speak unless you're spoken to." He tells me sternly. I remain silent as I let my head hang down as it takes too much energy to hold it up at this point. A few minutes pass before I hear a door open. I draw my head up and I see Mikhail enter the room.

"The boss will be arriving any minute, be on stand by." Mikhail tells the man. The man makes his way out the room, leaving me and Mikhail alone. He crouches down next to me and gives me a worried look. "Viktor knows." Mikhail tells me. "What?" I ask shocked. Surely he doesn't mean he knows about the mission. "I hate to see this outcome for you." Mikhail tells me genuinely. "It's not too late. You can still help us." I tell him. He lets out a sigh and hangs his head in defeat. "I wish I could, but I cannot risk my daughters safety. She's all I have now." Mikhail says. I give him a nod of understanding and he rises up and takes his spot by the door.

A few minutes later Viktor busts through the door with eight of his men who are all equipped with guns, including Nicholai and Dimitri. "My, my. What unfortunate circumstances it is for you Stella." Viktor says. I hide my dismay as I reply, "I don't know what you're talking about." I tell him. "Don't patronize me!" Viktor shouts. He circles around me as he rubs his hands to together and gives me a malicious smile. "I would've had fun with you." He tells me. "You're sick." I shout. He laughs, "Just wait until Liam joins us and finds out this is all a set up." Liam? That must be Derek's real name. I wiggle my wrists back and forth in hopes of triggering the alarm on my watch. At least he will be able to save himself and get to the extraction point before they realize it. I finally feel the mini shock my watch gives off to let me know the alarm has been signaled. Now I just have to keep him distracted long enough to keep his mind off Derek.

"What gave it away?" I ask him in Russian. He emits a pleased smile as if to say *I knew it.* "You forget, I have eyes everywhere. I have many clients in America willing to do some digging for me." I give him a look of disgust. "Don't worry. Your little act was quite convincing, but the GACF's firewalls don't stand a chance for the people I have on my payroll." He boasts. "So what now?" I ask him. "I think you know how this ends." Viktor says as he snaps his fingers. Nicholai approaches me and flips out his knife. He gives me a toothy grin as he rubs his blade along my cheek. "I'm going to enjoy every bit of this." He tells me. I deliver another spit to his face and he lets out an angry growl as he draws back his knife. "Nicholai!" Viktor shouts. Nicholai quickly stops and turns to face Viktor. "She keeps disrespecting me boss." Nicholai nearly whines. "Save it till our guest of honor joins us." Viktor tells him. Viktor gives him a nod as he resumes his composure.

I see Viktor glance at the clock on the wall and then whisper to one of his men. I can't help but feel pleased to know that Derek got the warning and know that Viktor doesn't get the satisfaction of killing us both. "What's wrong?" I ask Viktor with a smirk. I see his face become red and flustered. He quickly hobbles his way over to me and gives me a strong back hand. "Where is he?" He shouts. I spit the blood from my mouth, "Wouldn't you like to know." I say followed by a delirious laugh. Viktor gives a snarl and flicks his hand in the air. "Kill her, but slowly." He tells them and as he walks away, his men close in on me. Nicholai is the first to approach me and gives me a smug look before stabbing his knife into my thigh. I grit my teeth as I hold back a cry of pain. I'll be damned if I give him the satisfaction of causing me pain.

Nicholai withdraws the knife and is about deliver another stab to my leg when a loud crash comes from the far window. The men scatter and take cover throughout the warehouse. I hear three gunshots come from outside and then the breaking of another window. This time followed by a smoke screen. Everyone starts to choke from the suffocating smoke. The door swings open and I see Derek swiftly enter the room and toss a canister to the middle of the room and it emits a flash bang. His line of sight hones in on me and he runs over to me and quickly cuts my legs and hands free. We both run to a nearby pallet for cover and try to catch our breath.

I look at him and despite how glad I am to see him I can't help but get pissed at him. "Why did you come?" I hiss. "The thought of leaving you behind, I just couldn't." He tells me conflictingly. I give him a kiss, "Let's get out of here." I tell him. He nods and hands me the gun. "What about you?" I ask. "I'll be fine, now go." He tells me. He throws another smoke screen and we both make a run for the next pallet. Stray bullets are flying everywhere but, I manage to take down one guy along our way. As the smoke starts to settle again, I can see that about five hundred feet stand between us and freedom. I feel Derek tap my shoulder and I turn to see him motion to the far side of the wall. I know what he's thinking. It'll be safer to scale along the perimeter, but will take longer to get out. We crouch between the shelves and slowly make our way to the far wall. As we round the corner we run into one of the guys. I go to shoot him, but my gun clicks. I'm out of ammo. Shit. He raises his gun to shoot, but Derek kicks the back of his knees, taking him down to the ground. I use the end of the gun and knock him out.

"Over here." I hear a voice shout. We turn around to see a guy signaling others over. "Run." Derek tells me. We zig zag through the shelves and pallets as we make a run for the door. We are less than fifty feet from the door when I trip over an outstretched foot. As I fall to the ground, Nicholai emerges from behind a pallet and towers over me with a gun pointed to my head. I sweep his legs out from under him causing him to miss his shot and I crawl on top of him. I wrestle him for the gun which sends a few more bullets astray. I finally knock the gun out of his grasp and deliver a punch to his face and I can feel his nose crack under my fist. He grabs ahold of my throat and squeezes till I can hardly breathe. As I float in and out of consciousness, I remember one of the last moves Hitoshi taught. I use all my force to throw myself back and break free from his grip. I roll away and quickly grab the gun and pull the trigger which puts a bullet in Nicholai's head. I toss the gun aside and quickly rise to my feet and run to the door. "We made it!" I say relieved, as I fling open the door. I glance back at Derek, but isn't behind me. I turn around as I begin to panic. I scan the room and I see Derek laying a few feet from Nicholai's body. I feel my heart sink to the bottom of my stomach as I run to his side.

"Derek." I cry. He looks up at me as starts to sputter some blood when tries to smile. I look down and see a bullet hole to his chest and one to his stomach. I frantically try to apply pressure to his wounds and he takes my hands in his. "Go." He whispers. "You'll die." I croak, as I start to cry. He uses his thumb to wipe away my tears, "Death for you would be an honor." He tells me. I start to sob, "Now go." He adds. I look up and see the men coming around the corner and I give him a quick kiss before I get up and make a run for the door.

Once I make it out the door I keep running and I don't look back. I welcome the burning sensation as it fills my lungs. I run for about two miles before I tuck off into an alley to catch my breath. I start to cry once again and as the anguish settles in my stomach, I throw up. I wipe my mouth and look at my watch. I only have half a mile to go.

Chapter 15: Stella

The next four days are a blur. Once I make it back to the states they take me directly to medical to have me looked over and treated. I had to stay in for an additional three days to be monitored while I detoxed. I had to tell the nurse to not let any more visitors in because everyone was wanting to come in and congratulate me on the success of the mission. Apparently, Derek had managed to put a tracker on Chubinsky earlier that day and when he fled the scene they were able to catch up to him shortly after. I can't sit by and listen to other people give me credit for what Derek did. It pains me too much.

Kat hasn't left my side since I've been back and I can't be any more grateful for her support. She's the only one who I've disclosed all of the details to and she hasn't judged me one bit. This is why I love her like a sister. Mason has sent me flowers everyday and I don't know whether to be annoyed or appreciative. Ron has stopped by twice. Once initially to check on me and see how I was doing, and then another to inform me that debriefing will be postponed until further notice.

When they finally release me home, Ron has me under orders to be off duty for an entire month. Kat practically had to drag me out of there before I gave Ron a piece of my mind. "Don't worry, I've taken this whole month off too so we can have some long over due sisterly bonding time." Kat tells me once we get in the car. "You didn't have to do that." I tell her. "Hush, I wanted to." She tells me as she pats my hand.

As the weeks pass I submit myself to the torture of watching sappy romance movies and looking through the pictures of me and Derek. Kat gives me a look of concern as she looks over at me while I'm divulging in my very own gallon of ice cream. "That's it!" She says as she yanks the tub of ice cream from me. "Hey!" I say. "I can't just sit by and watch you destroy yourself. This isn't you." She tells me. I look away ashamed, because I know she's right. "You don't understand." I tell her. She scoots next to me and holds my hands in hers. "You're right. I don't, but you can't keep blaming yourself Stella." She tells me. "If I would have just agreed to abort the mission when he wanted to, we both would still be alive right now." I tell her as I start to cry. She pulls me into a hug. "He knew the risk when he back for you." She tells me. "It's still not fair." I tell her. "Why don't you get what's really hurting you, off your chest?" She says. "What do you mean?" I say defensively as I pull away. She gives me a stern look as I look back her dumbfounded. "I think we both know that this isn't just a typical feeling of guilt. You two shared a special bond and I think you need to admit how you felt about him." I stand up abruptly, "What do you want me to say Kat? You want me to tell you that I loved him? The one guy that I ever managed to love is now dead. Does it make you happy to hear me say it aloud?" She purses her lips to hold back her initial response. "No Stella it doesn't make me happy to see my best friend hurting and to know there's nothing I can do about it. But if you could at least be honest with yourself about your feelings then maybe you can finally start to cope." She tells me and then rises from her seat. "I'm going to bed." She mutters and then shuts herself in her room, I'm left standing there with nothing but my thoughts. I never really let myself believe that it was love I felt for Derek. After all, love is for sissies. At least that's what I thought.

The next morning I get up early so I can make us breakfast. When Kat finally emerges from her room she gives me an astonished look. "What the heck is all this?" She asks. I give a pitiful shrug, "An apology for being an ass. I know you were just trying to help." I tell her. She peers into the skillet and gives me a mischievous side eye. "If your cooking doesn't kill me, then apology accepted." She says teasingly. I elbow her as we both erupt with laughter.

The last two weeks end up flying by since I wasn't moping about as much, but I'd be lying if I said I didn't think of Derek often. I feel slightly anxious about returning to work, but also anticipating my return. I feel that if I stayed one more day in this house, then I might just go ballistic with cabin fever.

The day of my return, I get dressed and meet Kat as she offered to go in late so she could drive me. When we make it to the agency everyone gives a friendly nod, smile, or wave as I pass by. Once we make it to my office, Kat gives me a small hug. "Text me if you need anything." She tells me. "I will." I reply as I give her a parting smile. As I get settled back in my office, it's not long before there's a soft knock at the door.

"Come in." I say and watch as Mason enters the office. "Hi Stella." He says. "Hi Mason." I reply. "How are you feeling?" "I'm alright." I tell him. "I was really worried about you. Especially when they relayed that your cover alarm was signaled, ya know?" I know what he's trying to say without saying it. Usually whoever activates the alarm doesn't have a happy ending. "Well, lucky me. I'm still here." I say a little more rudely than I meant to. He rubs the back of his neck nervously. "Um, yeah. Anyways I just wanted to stop and say hi." He says and turns to leave. "Mason." I call out. He spins around and looks at me, "Thank you for the flowers." I tell him followed by a half smile. He gives me a soft smile, "You're welcome." He says and then disappears.

The next hour I spend sifting through paperwork and feel myself on the brink of boredom when another knock at my door is welcomed. This time it's Ron. "Think you might be up for some debriefing?" He inquires. I feel a lump in my throat form as I know it'll be required to discuss what happened to Derek. I give him a s simple nod to show my unwillingness, but that I'll do it anyway. "Good. Conference room, five minutes." I set aside what I'm working on and retrieve my mission file and make my way to the conference room.

As I enter the room, I see a bunch of reps from each department along with Ron and Randall. Randall rises from his seat and sticks out his hand and I give him a firm handshake. I couldn't imagine what it would be like to lose an agent. The GACF has been pretty lucky these last five years. I take my seat as Ron starts to go over details that we accumulated during our time there. Once he goes over all the formalities he asks if I want to review the footage that I captured the night I spoke with Nadia. I decline the opportunity to save myself the embarrassment. They review it regardless, I just don't want to be present when they do so. That's the night I let my emotions get the best of me and I slapped Derek. I already know that'll be a critique point.

"Anything you'd like to address?" Ron asks Randall. Randall rises from his chair. "Yes. I just want to say thank you for the GACF's collaboration on this mission and we are thrilled to put Viktor Chubinsky and four of his men away. We appreciate your thoughts and concerns during this time, but we are pleased to announce that agent Morrison awoke from his coma early this morning." Everyone starts to clap and it's as if I'm experiencing shell shock. I suddenly become nauseous and sweaty. Derek is alive. "Y-y-you mean the man who was my partner?" I verify. "Yes. He suffered some serious injuries and we weren't sure if he was going to pull through or not, but I'll be damned, he's a tough cookie." Randall says. I feel like my heart just might explode. I have to see him. "Where is he?" I ask. Ron gives me a stern look, "Agent Parks, you know that is against protocol." Just like that, my heart finds itself in the pit of my stomach once more. "Right. I apologize, you know I'm not use to working with a partner." I say. "Will we have to meet again so he can debrief?" I ask curiously. "Given the circumstances, agent Morrison would benefit more from focusing on his healing at this time. If he feels he should need to debrief we will reconvene at that time." Randall tells me. "Very well. Thank you for the update." I tell him. "Are we done here?" I add. Ron gives me a nod and I excuse my self.

I return to my office and start to pace. My heart is pounding with excitement. I can't believe he's alive. I try to think of a way to see him. I know nothing about him because of our stupid rules. That's not true, I know his real name. Liam Morrison. Where do I even start looking? I think to myself. That's when a lightbulb goes off in my head. I text Kat. *Call me ASAP.*

A minute later my phone starts to ring. "Stella, is everything okay?" Kat asks. "He's alive Kat! Derek is alive! I just found out during debrief." I tell her excitedly. "Oh my God! That is unbelievable. Where is he?" "I don't know. They aren't allowed to say and it's killing me." I tell her. "Damn. Too bad you don't have any of his information." She tells me. "Well…" I say menacingly. "Stella, just tell me." She says. "Liam Morrison, that's his name. That's all I know, well and the fact he's with the FBI." "Got it. I'll get back to you." She says and hangs up.

I try to sit down and continue where I left off before the debriefing, but I can't concentrate. I'm too anxious to focus and keep looking at my phone. I put my head down on my desk and let out a large sigh. I feel my phone buzz and I quickly look at it. Kat: *Washington Memorial Hospital.* Before I can even reply she forwards me the address. Stella: *You're the best! I'll be back in a couple days.* I reply. Kat: *Safe travels, XOXO.* She replies. I grab my bag and head straight to Ron's office.

I knock on his door and wait for him to welcome me in. "Stella, to what do I owe the pleasure?" He says. If he knew where I was really going I would lose my job, so I decide to lie. "I can't do this today. This is too much sir." I tell him frantically. He stands up and comes over to me. "Hey it's okay. If you need more time then take it." He tells me compassionately. "I just hate to seem weak." I tell him. "No one has to know." He tells me. It pains me to lie to Ron, he's been nothing but good to me, but this way he can claim plausible deniability. "Why don't you go ahead and call it a day?" He tells me. "Okay." I say giving him a sullen nod. After I leave Ron's office, I pass the elevator and practically sprint down the stairs. Once I make it to the street, I fetch a cab and head straight to the airport.

I don't make it to D.C. till the next day and decide to get a hotel room first, so I can freshen up before I go to the hospital. Once I shower and change into the adorable outfit I picked up from the boutique next door, I catch a cab to the hospital. When the cab pulls up, I feel my heart start to beat faster. I pay the man and hop out, anxious to get inside.

"Hi how can I help?" The receptionist asks. "Could you tell me what floor Liam Morrison is on?" I ask. "He's on floor five, our critical care unit. You'll need to check in with them before they give you his room number." "Okay, thank you." I tell her. I take the closet elevator up to the fifth floor and make my way to the nurse's desk.

"Hello. Who are you here to see?" The nurse asks. "Liam Morrison." I reply. She grabs a clipboard off the desk. "Your name?" I stare at her for a moment, unsure of how to respond. "Stella Parks, but he knows me as Emma Matthews." I tell her. She looks at me suspiciously before looking over the clipboard. "I'm sorry. You're not on the visitor list, so I can't give you his room number." I've come too far to be defeated now. I put my hands down on the desk and lean towards her. "I know you know his story. I was his partner and I just need to see that he's okay." I beg. "Please." I add desperately. She looks at me and then gives a defeating sigh. "Fine. Just make it quick." She tells me. I give her a nod. "527." She says as she point down the hallway to the right. "Thank you so much." I tell her.

I feel my steps grow faster with each room I pass and I can feel my heart beating uncontrollably. I can't wait to tell him how I feel. The selfish part of me wants him to be awake, but I know he needs his rest. If he's asleep though, I'll wait however long it takes for him to wake up. 525, 526, and here it is 527 I think to myself as I arrive in front of his door. I look through the blinds and see a young blonde woman laying in bed with him. I can't hear what she's saying, but I see her talking to him as she runs her fingers through his hair. Who is this woman? I think angrily. "Are you here to see Liam?" I hear a man's voice ask. I turn around to see a slightly older couple behind me. The man looks like an older, well-aged version of Liam so I can only assume these are his parents. "Oh, um. I was just coming by to say hi, but it looks like now isn't a good time." I say. The woman lets out a chuckle. "Don't be silly. I'm sure he won't mind a break from his fiancé's incessant talking. That's all she's done since he woke up." She tells me. His fiancé? I feel the hallway start to spin. How could he have sex with me and practically tell me he loves me, when he was engaged this whole time? I look over at him one last time as I feel my heart shatter. I give them a polite smile, "That's quite alright. I'll come back later." I tell them and turn to make my quick escape. As I round the nurse's desk, I dart into the bathroom and shove my way into the stall, just in time for me to throw up. I start to cry once the anger and hurt builds up. I'm so angry, I could scream. I take a couple deep breaths and go to the sink to splash my face with some cold water before exiting the bathroom.

I take my loss and catch the next flight back to Virginia. I feel humiliated and heart broken. I can't believe the nerve of him. This is exactly why I have always stuck to myself. It was all just a stupid lie, I should've known better. After all, you can't ever get let down if never get your hopes up in the first place. Maybe this is why the GACF has their protocols in place, for the idiots like me that get played.

I am relieved once I finally make it back home. As I enter the house, I hear Kat call out. "Stella?" She says as she rounds the corner. I look at her and my lip begins to quiver. "That bastard has a fiancé!" I shout. "Oh hunny." She says as she comes over and embraces me in a big hug. "I think this calls for some wine, yeah?" She says to me. I just nod as I cry into her shoulder.

I give myself the next two days to cope and recover from my hangover before returning to work. When I finally show up to work I beg Ron to assign me something other than desk work, because I can't be alone with my thoughts.

Not right now anyway. So, he agrees to let me take over the role as primary instructor for the training course. Which means I'll be working alongside Mason, just like old times. Of course when I tell Mason the news, he is thrilled and offers to go over some of the new tactics with me before the next training session.

Over the next couple of weeks I do my best to fit back into my training role. Although I'm still faster and wittier than Mason and our aspiring agents, I can't help but notice how many mistakes I make. Not to mention, how much slower my times have been too. It just makes me all the more determined to push myself even more.

As we get ready to take a new round of trainees into the course, I try to brush off the headache I'm feeling. The two trainees join Mason and I and we wait for the simulation to begin. A loud bang signals the start and the room begins to quickly feel with fog, which is supposed to emulate a smoke screen. We each pull out our masks and put them on before advancing to our next cover point. We stay in circle formation to watch each others back and just as we are about to make it to our cover point I start to get lightheaded. I quickly take off my mask, but it doesn't help as now the room looks as if it's spinning. I try to call out to Mason, but it's too late, I collapse to the ground and that's the last thing I remember.

When I wake up, I recognize that I'm down in medical. Mason is sitting at the edge of the bed and gives me a big smile once he see's that I'm awake. "Hey how are you feeling?" He asks. "My head is throbbing." I tell him. "What happened?" I ask. "You passed out during training, you had everyone worried sick." He tells me. I let out a groan as I smother myself with the pillow. "How embarrassing." I say.

Bailey, the lead doctor down in medical approaches me. "Stella, so glad to see you're awake." "Thanks doc. So what's all this about?" I ask her as I hold up my arm which has an IV with fluids running through it. "You were pretty dehydrated. You really should be drinking plenty of water and not overexerting your body Stella. It's not healthy for the baby." Me and Mason both give her a shocked look. "Excuse me. The what?" I ask, to ensure I heard her clearly. "I'm so sorry Stella, I thought you knew." She tells me as her face becomes riddled with guilt. "I'm pregnant?" I say. "Yes, it sure looks that way. Approximately two and a half months along." She tells me. This can't be, I think to myself. That means it would be Liam's baby. I look over at Mason and I already know he has put two and two together. "How is this possible? I get the birth control shots regularly, I haven't missed a single dose or ever been late." "They aren't a hundred percent effective Stella, there is always the possibility." "Yeah, but this never hap…" I start to say, but trail off. I realize now that even when we hooked up, I still always made Mason wear a condom because I wanted to protect myself from any STD's. Which now that I think about my one moment of weakness, I was so caught up in the moment and filled with passion and adrenaline that I succumbed to temptation. Now I start to worry. If he could do such a thing while being engaged, then who knows what else he could be hiding. "Would you mind adding some STD tests?" I ask Bailey. I look over at Mason and I can tell he's somewhere between uncomfortable, but also hurt. "Sure, no problem. We'll need to do some swabs though which means you'll need to step out agent Palmer." She says to Mason. Mason doesn't hesitate as he gets up and quietly leaves the room.

Once I'm released from medical I make my way back to my office to gather my things. For some reason, I feel like I owe Mason an explanation and decide to stop by his cubicle. "Hi." I say. He looks up from his computer and gives me an awkward smile. "Hi." He says. "Do you have a minute?" I ask him. I can see the reluctance on his face, but he obliges anyway. He follows me to my office and I wait until the door is securely shut before I start talking. I spend the next thirty minutes explaining what happened, without going into the finer details of that night.

As I lay it all out in the open, reality starts to hit me. My career is all I have, and if Ron finds out, I'm done for. I go over to him, "Mason, please, you can't tell anyone. I beg you." I say. He pulls me into a hug, "Your secret is safe with me." He whispers. "Thank you." I say as I start to cry. "You do have to realize though, this isn't something you can hide for much longer." He tells me. "I know. I just need time to think of my options." I tell him. "Are you going to tell him?" Mason asks. I become momentarily enraged as I shove myself away from him. "No, because apparently he has a fiancé." I say angrily. I watch as Mason's mouth falls slightly open and then wrenches in disgust. "What a fucking tool." Mason says. "Right?" I tell him. "I mean, you can still tell him, and see how he reacts. That way you at least see his true colors." He says. "Why bother? Besides what if he wants to share custody or try to take full custody? I'd be a single mom and they would be an established family. The court always rules in their favor." I start to rattle. "I was an orphan. I don't know what it's like to love or care for another human being. How do I even know if I'm fit to be a mom?" Mason puts his hands on my shoulders. "Breathe." He tells me before adding, "You would be a great mom, because you excel at everything you do. If you don't want to tell him, then that's your choice. You always know how to make the decisions that are best for you." Now I start to feel guilty because I know, his last words are in reference to me calling off our fling. "Thank you Mason. It's just so scary and foreign territory for me. I don't want to tell him, because why should he get the best of worlds and have the happy ending? But I also don't want to be alone during this either." I tell him conflictingly. He looks at me and gives me a soft smile. "You won't be alone. You have me, and of course Kat too." He tells me. Oh shit, I totally forgot about Kat. She is going to flip when I tell her. I give him a warm smile as the outlook doesn't seem so dim now. "You're right. Thank you Mason."

Once I get home, I tell Kat the news and she takes it dramatically well. She is already rattling off different names and has proclaimed herself as *Aunt Kat*. She even refused to discuss me moving out and insists that we just convert the office into the baby's room. Talking about it with her definitely gets me more excited and hopeful about the whole ordeal.

The next couple of weeks I spend going to follow up appointments and attending first time mother classes. I never pictured myself as a parent, but now that the reality is here, I want to be the best mom I can be. I've read numerous books and have done hours of research about the birthing process and child development. As far as work, I've respectfully pulled myself from the training position and been more adamant about my desk work. Even though it pains me, I plan to submit a request to transfer back to the Operations department. This way I can still work for the GACF, because the work isn't as physically tolling. Plus, it's a job I can keep while raising my child, with less potential threats to our safety too.

As the weeks have passed, I've grown more excited to be a mom and I don't think I'd be willing to share that role with a man I apparently barely know and his soon to be wife. So, I've decided against telling Liam. Besides, there's no sense in disrupting his life and relationship. Not that I should be worrying about his happiness, but I think part of me is afraid of how he would react. News like this could ruin his relationship, and then what, he end up resenting our child? It's not a chance I am willing to take. I can already feel my mentality evolving, as the safety and happiness of my unborn child is now what gives my life purpose. Being a spy was thrilling and fun, but knowing I'm going to be a mom is just as exhilarating and nerve wrecking. I can't wait to see what the future holds.

Chapter 16: Liam

Today marks almost three months since we were
extracted from Russia and only two months since I woke up
from my coma. For the life of me I can't understand how I
survived, given the injuries I sustained. While Emma and
Nicholai were wrestling for the gun, stray bullets fired off,
with one going into my chest and another into my stomach.
The one in my chest ended up collapsing my right lung while
the other bullet nicked a portion of my small intestine. They
think the amount of blood I lost from my abdominal wound
is what sent me into the coma.

Since I woke up, all I've been able to think about is
Emma and how she is doing. Hell I swore I even saw her
standing outside my hospital room one day, but with the
amount of drugs they had me on, who knows what I saw.
Seeing her again is what's motivated and pushed me to get
through rehab and recovery. Now that I'm projected to be
released this week, I am already planning a trip to Virginia. I
know it's against the GACF's protocols, but to hell with their
rules. There's nothing like being on the brink of death to
make a person realize what they want in life, and for me,
that's Emma.

When I'm released from the hospital, Ma and Pa
thought it would be a good idea to throw me a welcome
home party. Despite politely declining their offer, they of
course did it anyway and now I'm having to prepare myself
to be bombarded with a bunch of people who don't really
give a damn about me. Ma and Pa have been pushing me
now more than ever to propose to Anna. They think that my

miraculous recovery is a sign for a fresh start and I shouldn't be taking my life for granted. Although, I agree, Anna is not the person I want to spend the rest of my life with. I can barely stand being in the same room with her for longer than thirty minutes, how could I live with her? Emma on the other hand, I could spend an eternity with her and it still wouldn't be enough.

"Babeeee!" I hear Anna screech as we enter the house. This prompts the large group of people standing in the foyer to turn and applaud. As I pass through crowd I get a bunch of pats on the shoulder and *welcome home's*. I finally make it upstairs to put my things in my old room, when I hear my door shut. I turn to see Anna with a seductive grin on her face.

"Yes Anna?" I say gruffly as I continue to unpack. "Boy have I missed you." She tells me as she comes behind me and starts to caress my back. I remain silent, because I don't wanna lie and tell her that I feel the same. I hear the sound of a zipper and then feel Anna tap on my shoulder. I turn to find her dress fallen to the ground and she's left standing in her bra and panties. "What are you doing?" I ask her. "I thought we could have a little fun before you go back down." She tells me as she approaches me and then pulls me toward her. I pull away from her, "Damn it Anna, put your dress back on." I tell her firmly. "Don't you think it's the least you could do? You just run off all dark and mysterious and then end up in a coma. Do you know what I have gone through while you were away?" She spouts off. I grit my teeth at her annoying self pity demeanor. "Please enlighten me Anna." I tell her.

"Well for starters, I had to go to Miranda's birthday party stag. This is the second event I had to go to solo, now everyone is spreading rumors that I'm lying about dating you. Secondly, you didn't even send a gift to makeup for it, like rude. Then you didn't send a gift for our seven month anniversary, or our eighth, but I'll let that one slide since you were in a coma." "Do you even hear yourself when you talk?" I say, cutting her off. "Excuse me?" She says. "You are the most selfish and self centered person I know. I don't even know how I've been with you this long." I tell her. "Pfft. Do you know how many guys would kill to be with me? You're lucky I let you be with me." "Yeah well if that's the case, I'd much rather be the unlucky one." I tell her. "What are you trying to say Liam?" I throw my hands up in frustration, "I'm saying we're done. I don't want to be with you anymore. We're breaking up. I don't know how else to get the message across." I tell her. Her face scrunches up in rage as she pulls up her dress and storms out the room. "Good riddance." I mutter. Breaking up with Anna was long overdue, but it needed to be done. It's only a matter of time before Ma and Pa find out, so I plop down on the bed and wait for my intervention to take place.

After about half an hour there's soft knock on my door and Pa emerges. He makes his way over and takes a seat on the edge of the bed. "So you broke up with Anna I hear?" He says. I continue to stare at the ceiling, "Yeah, long over due." I tell him. I feel him give small chuckle, "Yeah I supposed it was, wasn't it." "I just don't get why you and Ma would want me to be with someone like that in the first place." Pa lets out a sigh, "I think your mom was convinced that Anna was a good match because politically, you two complimented each other." "Yeah, but you know I don't care about any of that stuff. Besides, you're supposed to marry for love and all that warm fuzzy shit." I tell him. "Indeed. That's why I'm honestly relieved you did what you did." Pa tells me. "You are?" I ask, a bit confused. He lets out another small chuckle, "Yes, I am. After all, it might give you and that girl at the hospital a chance to work things out." He tells me. I instantly shoot up, "What girl at the hospital?" I ask him. "Hm, I don't think we got her name. Cute red head though, she came to see you, but Anna was in with you and she didn't wanna intrude." Shit. Emma probably thinks I'm the biggest asshole on the planet. I jump out of bed and start repacking my bag. "What are you doing?" Pa asks. "I have to go see her." I tell him. "Son, you just got out of the hospital. I'm sure she would understand." "No, you don't understand. She was my partner, and now after seeing Anna, she probably thinks I took advantage of her." I say stressfully. "Ah, well yes. That is a bit of a problem." He tells me. "Are you sure it can't wait? We just got you back." He asks. I look at him and throw my hands up in the air, "I love her Pa." He gives me a smile and nods his head. "Then go get your girl." He tells me. I give him a big smile and zip up my bag and run down the stairs.

I didn't even stop to say bye to Ma, but I'm sure Pa will fill her in. I came straight to the airport and booked the first flight to Virginia. I feel excited and nervous all at the same time. I can only imagine how pissed she is at me and can only hope she will forgive me. I hope she's been doing okay. I can't wait to hold her again and tell her how I feel. The pessimist in me keeps worrying that she may not feel the same way. Why would she disobey the protocols to find me and come see me then? She has to feel the same way too.

I have no idea how to get in touch with her so I do the only thing I know to do. The next morning I show up to the GACF and see if I can find her. After going through clearance, I take the elevators up to the floor I know she works on. "Hi there. Could you help me find one of your agents?" I ask as I approach the receptionist. "Sure, what's their name?" She asks. "Well that's the thing. We were on a mission together recently so I don't know her real name, but I was hoping to find that out." I tell her. "I'm really sorry, but that is against protocol 6.2. Unless you already know her name, I can't disclose it to you." She tells me. Now I'm starting to get irritated. "Can I just walk around and see if I see her then? I know she works on this floor." I say. "You can, but it won't do you much good. That particular agent doesn't work in this department anymore." She says. "What?" I say a bit baffled. "Then why can't you just throw me a bone here?" I tell her. "I'm really sorry, I can't help you." She tells me. Feeling frustrated and defeated, I make my way back to the elevator.

"Hold the elevator!" I hear a man shout. I wait for him to get on and then hit the button. "Thanks." He says and I give him a nod. Once the elevator shuts, I get a sucker punch right to the stomach, taking me down to my knees. Followed by a knee the face. What the hell is going? Given that he socked me right where the bullet to my abdomen hit, I can't even muster the breath to talk. He crouches down and gets close my face, "Stay away, she doesn't want to see you." He tells me seethingly. The elevator dings and he quickly stands up. "Oh my God Mason, what happened?" I hear a girl say as she rushes to my side to evaluate the damage. "I'm fine." I manage to say as I look up at her. "Wait, I know you." She says. "You do?" I say puzzled, as I have never met this woman before. "You're Liam, the one who went on the mission with…" "Don't!" Mason shouts cutting the woman off." "What is your deal?" She says to Mason, "He doesn't know her true identity. I'd hate to report you for breaking protocol Kat." She gives him a glare. "This isn't our fight Mason." She tells hims. I manage to pull myself together and stand. "I just need to talk to her so I can explain." I say. "You had your chance." Mason says harshly. "Really? In the middle of a mission, don't you think that would break protocol?" I tell him sarcastically. "That didn't stop you from screwing her though." He spouts. "Mason!" Kat yells. "Dude, I admit. It wasn't the wisest decision, but I'm trying to make things right here." I tell him. The elevator finally reaches the first floor and opens up. "You would've been better off staying dead." Mason says as he exits the elevator. I look over at the woman named Kat and give her a look of defeat. "You don't have to tell me anything. If you'll just give her a message for me." She gives me a nod. "Will you tell her I love her? Tell her that all of my feelings were true and that there hasn't been a second that's passed since I met her that I haven't thought about her." I say. "You're putting me in a tough spot here. She's finally happy again, and now you're asking me to turn her world upside down again." Kat tells me. I take a hard swallow at my harsh reality. "I understand. I only want her to be happy and even if that's without me then I'll suck it up." I tell her before walking off. "Wait!" She shouts. I turn around to face her as she lets out a large sigh. "Give me your phone number and I'll see what I can do." She tells me. I feel my face light up like a Christmas tree. "Really?" I ask. She holds up her hand, "No guarantees though." She tells me and I give her an understanding nod. I type my number in her phone and hand it back. "I can't thank you enough." I tell her followed by a hug. I'm not usually so excitable, but when it comes to this, I can't seem to hide my emotions.

Kat

I usually try not to get involved in other people's business, but I can tell Liam's feelings for Stella are genuine. She is more than just my best friend, she is my sister, and I would be doing her a disservice if I just sat by and didn't give her the option to be truly happy. I'm still leaving it up to her though, because it's her life not mine. I know she's at an appointment right now so I patiently wait for her to get out before I call.

"Hey girl, you must be psychic. I just got done and was about to call you." Stella says. "Well how did it go?" I ask. "So far so good. The little bean's growth is right on track." She tells me. "That's great news! So you're still waiting to know the gender?" I say. I hear her laugh, "At least for now. You know I'll probably cave eventually." She says. "You are crazy. I couldn't do it for one day." I tell her. "Well, I think I'm gonna stop for a coffee before I head home, decaf of course. Would you like anything?" She asks me. "You and your coffee." I tell her teasingly. "Sure, just get me my usual." I add. "Great, see you soon." She tells me. "Stella wait." I say frantically. "What is it Kat?" She says and I can sense the worry in her voice. "Liam was at the agency today. He was looking for you." I tell her. "You didn't tell him did you?" She asks. "Well of course not. He doesn't even know your real name and I almost let it slip, but Mason stopped me." I tell her. "Mason? What the hell. Where were you at?" She asks. "I take it Mason cornered him in the elevator and gave him a decent threatening to stay away. It's a good thing I was getting on the elevator or who knows what else Mason would've done to him." I say. "Is he okay?" Stella asks. "Yeah I think he'll be alright." I tell her. "That's it I'm going to call Mason and give him a piece of my mind. I don't need people fighting my battles for me." She says and I can tell she's starting to get worked up. "I think you should meet with Liam though. I think you'll want to hear what he has to say." I tell her. "Pfft. I don't care what he has to say." She tells me. "Stella then at least let me tell you what he told me." I plead. "No! I will not sit back and be anyone's second choice or side piece. I have more self respect for myself than that and I will not subject my child to a life of constant back and forth turmoil." She says. "Fine. I understand." I tell her. "Thank you. I'll see you soon." She says and hear the phone click.

Sheesh, she can be so hard headed sometimes, I think to myself. I don't want to defy Stella's wishes, but I think if she just saw him, then she would give him a chance. How can I get her to see him, without blatantly breaking her trust? Then it dawns on me, I know just what to do.

Liam

I spend the next hour pacing my hotel room and incessantly checking my phone. I hope Emma will at least give me a chance to explain. And if I can just see her, then I can tell her how I feel. I practice rehearsing what I want to say when I see her, but I already know once I see her, I'm going to forget everything. I hear my phone vibrate and I rush over to the night stand to check it. It's Kat: *I'm sorry, she doesn't want to see you.* I feel my heart shatter into a million pieces as I read her words. I throw my phone across the room and let out a frustrated growl. I'm such an idiot. What did I think was going to happen? Did I really think I'd be able to just come here and pick up where we left off? I fall onto the bed and let out a large sigh in hopes of keeping the tears away. I hear my phone buzz once more and I reluctantly get up and retrieve it off the floor. Kat again: *Maybe you should get a coffee and regroup*, she suggests. I let out a scoff, I can't even think about coffee without thinking of Emma. Maybe Kat is right though, a coffee may be just what I need to recharge and think of a new plan.

When I make it to the local coffee shop, I order my coffee and sullenly take my seat in the back corner as I try to think of my other options. I could stake the building, but that is just outright creepy and stalkerish. I'm about to accept defeat when I hear the door ding and I look up to see Emma walk in. I hold my breath as I watch her walk to the counter and give the barista her dazzling smile. Then it hits me, Kat must've known she was coming here. Ugh, she is an angel in disguise. I get up and try to make my way over to her, but it's as if my legs are molasses. I stand from a distance as she places her order, and it makes me wonder who she's getting coffee for because neither are her usual order. What if she's moved on? It would explain why that asshat, Mason was so protective.

When she turns around and sees me she lets out a little gasp and stops in her tracks. "Hi Emma." I say as I give her a half smile. She crosses her arms, "Jokes on you, that's not even my name." She says as she shoves her way past me. "Then how about we start over?" I say as I follow her. "What's the point?" She snaps. "So I can explain. I can tell you who I really am." I plead. "Oh I know exactly who you are, Liam Morrison. You're the type of guy who can have a fiancé, but still have sex with another woman and then go home to their fiancé like nothing even happened." She tells me in angry hushed whisper and I can see the hurt in her eyes and it kills me to know, I've caused her pain. "It's not even like that. She's not my fiancé." I tell her. "So your moms a liar?" She tells me furiously. Of course Ma, would tell her Anna was my fiancé. "Partly. My mom has been pushing me and Anna to get married, but we were never engaged. I detest her with every fiber of my being and I even told her I never want to see her again the day I was released." I say. She remains silent and I use this as my opportunity to express my feelings. "You are all that I have thought about since I woke up from my coma. I busted my ass in rehab, because I knew the sooner I got out, the sooner I'd be able to get back to you. I love you Emma, and I don't expect you to feel the same way, but I know you care about me or you wouldn't have broken protocol to come see me." I tell her. I see her bottom lip quiver and I can't help myself. I pull her into a hug and hold her tight. I can feel her crying into my chest and I offer a soothing kiss to the top of her head. After a long moment, she forcefully pushes herself away from me and gives me a punch to the chest. "Do you know what I have been through these past three months?" She tells me. I wipe away one of her tears, "I don't, but I'm here now." I tell her.

The barista calls out for a Stella, and I watch as her head swivels in his direction. "So your name is Stella." I say. She purses her lips to keep from smiling, but she caves. "There's that beautiful smile, I've missed so much." I tell her. I see her cheeks turn rosy as she looks away. I gently turn her head to look back at me and as I stare into her eyes. "I love you Stella." "I love you too." She whispers. I can't hold it back any longer, I kiss her and when I feel her kiss me back, it's as if I'm whole again.

"Well isn't this just cute." I hear a bitter familiar voice say. As we break away, I see Mason standing across from us. "Mason relax." Stella says. "No, this is bullshit. You were doing just fine without him." Mason says. "You're right. I don't have to be with Liam, but I'm choosing to. It's my life and it's my choice." She says. "You're not thinking clearly, don't let your emotions cloud your judgement." Mason tells her. "I think she's capable of thinking for herself." I tell him, starting to get slightly annoyed that he's interrupting our moment. He sneers at me, "Of course you'd find a way to weasel your way into her and the baby's life." Mason says angrily. "Mason!" Stella shouts. "Baby?" I ask shocked, as I look at her. Mason's face falls with embarrassment and Stella gives me a horrified look. "I-I was going to tell you." She stammers. "When? Because prior to a few minutes ago, you were content with never speaking to me again." I tell her. "What was she supposed to do? You have a fiancé." Mason interjects harshly. "Mason just shut up and leave." Stella says as she rubs her temples. Mason remains silent as he sulks away to leave.

"You're pregnant?" I ask as I still can't believe what I've heard. She lets out a sigh. "Yes, yes I am." "How far along?" I ask. "I'm twelve weeks and three days as of today." She tells me and I can't help but look down at her belly. "So that would mean it would definitely be..." I trail off. "Yours. Yes." She says, finishing my sentence. "Why wouldn't you tell me? Even if I did have a fiancé, you know I care about you too much to let you go through this alone." I tell her. "Because, why should you get the happily ever after? A house, a marriage, our kid, while I sit on the back burner and get labeled as the mother of a desperate love affair. I couldn't do it." She tells me. "You could never be on the back burner. You are too amazing, and beautiful, and brilliant, and let's not forget badass, to ever be second best." I tell her. This prompts a small laugh as she starts to cry once more. "You will forever be the one and only woman for me." I tell her as

I gaze into her eyes. She then pulls me into a long passionate kiss and I can tell this is the beginning of our forever, and I couldn't be happier.

Epilogue: Stella

The past five months have been quite eventful for me and Liam. A month after our reconciliation in the coffee shop, we got married. It was a beautiful secluded ceremony with our only guests being Kat and Liam's parents. At first I was leery about rushing into marriage, but Liam reassured me that it's not just cause I'm pregnant with his child. He said if he didn't think I would've shot him down, he would've proposed to me at the coffee shop before he even knew about the baby.

Given the circumstances, we got our own place together and I couldn't be happier. Sometimes I still can't believe that this is my life now. I got the man of my dreams who adores me and a perfect healthy little girl who will be arriving next month. I couldn't help it, I caved. But I don't regret my decision one bit. It's hilarious watching Liam come home with a new outfit, that he insists he couldn't pass up.

As for my job, I'm going to continue working under the Operations branch for now. Liam has already said that he knows how much my career means to me and has offered to step down as an agent so I can be an agent again once I'm ready. I told him we would approach that when the time comes. Right now, I just want to be the best mom I can be for Adelina. That's why I've confided in Liam about my past and how much it means to me for us to be one big happy family. Which I already know is Liam's main priority as well. Despite feeling like a blubbering whale, Liam makes me feel like the prettiest woman alive and continues to pamper me each day. Some days, I have to remind him that I'm a self sufficient woman. I know he just cares about me and our little girl and that's why there's not a day that goes by that I don't feel loved. I would've thought eventually that our intense passion and feelings would simmer down, but on the contrary. We can't keep our hands off one another and it's as if each day we fall more and more in love with each other.

Liam's parents have welcomed me with open arms and it's as if I have finally gotten the parents I thought I'd never have. It did take Mrs. Morrison a little while to warm up to me, but now she calls and video chats me everyday. They are excited for the arrival of their grand baby and have been working with Kat to ensure that me and Liam have everything we need.

It's crazy how a person can come into your life and change it just like that. I can't complain though. My life has changed so much for the better and I wouldn't change a single thing. Who would've thought that Stella Parks would get the happy ending? Oops, I mean Stella Morrison...

www.ingramcontent.com/pod-product-compliance
Lightning Source LLC
Chambersburg PA
CBHW052010240626
47153CB00008B/2816